I0788560

Hill City Press

Edited by Sara Lawson.

Jacket design by Everly Haywood.

Cover art by Lulybot.

Interior art by Lulybot.

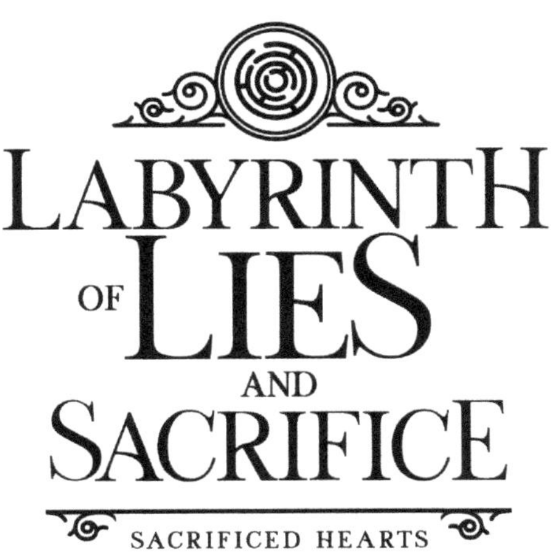

LABYRINTH OF LIES AND SACRIFICE

SACRIFICED HEARTS

C. F. E. BLACK

For those who feel trapped by their past.
May you find the key to set you free.

Sign up for reader VIP treatment including bonus content and sneak peeks at all new books by heading to cfeblack.com/pages/vip

1

Today, I was going to burn to death.

That one thought echoed through my mind as I raced through the meandering streets of Varich in the predawn gloom, a paper-wrapped parcel stuffed under my arm and my market bag bouncing against my hip. My dress, stained from where I'd spilled hot wax on it far past midnight, rustled and flapped like a circus tent in a strong wind. I'd given up trying to move silently and lunged into an all-out sprint—which was tricky when juggling a package containing my heavy wedding gown.

Or rather, the gown I'd wear to my wedding. I doubted I'd survive the fire mage marriage ceremony, considering I *wasn't* a fire mage.

This thought had kept me awake most of the night, sweating in my bed, considering and reconsidering all the awful ways this day would unfold. As I skittered around the corner beside the Guild's private club, my eyes traveled up to the single lit window shining out over the empty street. If anyone inside saw my pale face darting by, they'd likely make one of two wrong

1

assumptions: that I'd stolen the item I carried or that I was hustling home after an illicit night out. Either way, if someone was watching, they'd come for me.

And I couldn't afford to be questioned on why I was carrying a dress the color of ash—the color every woman wore to wed a fire mage.

A faint groaning drifted down the quiet street, and I glanced into the deep shadows under the grand arched entrance to the Guild's headquarters. A woman was on her knees, offering supplications to the magical elite. The woman, dressed in black, blended in with the shadows.

Heart racing as fast as a trapped mouse, I shoved my hand into my market bag, fumbled for the two apples rolling around, then scurried forward and set them carefully on the ground beside the beggar. She glanced back at me, eyes red from tears, then fell forward again in her rhythmic petitions. My heart sank. The mages who ran the Guild paraded around town like saviors in their color-coded robes and their fancy rings, doing the king's bidding and ensuring that the rest of us knew our place in life.

"They won't help you," I hissed at the woman, as I tried to cram the wedding dress back into my bag. Two months ago, the Guild had thrown her husband in the Labyrinth, a magical prison built by the king, for allegedly stabbing one of the king's guards; they weren't about to support his wife, even if she was most likely a widow by now.

I couldn't afford to loiter in front of the Guild, so I took off down the street once more. Guild members lived above the law in many cases and considered it their fate-gifted duty to assist the lawmen in meting out punishments of their own devising to petty criminals. I wasn't in the mood to parade around town in a pair of shackles or find a black X tattooed on my hand in the blink of an eye. I hadn't stolen anything, despite the fact that I was running like a thief in the darkened streets. Mother had paid for this dress with our own money—a testament to how much she wanted me to marry this stranger. But if a Guild member asked, I'd lie and say I just thought the dress was pretty enough to steal, because the alternative to being branded a thief was far worse.

If the Guild discovered I was to be married today, they'd send a representative from one of the magical affinities to observe the wedding. Since the war, all mage weddings were to be witnessed by the Guild, recorded for posterity, and the unions subsequently tracked for any progeny. All mages had to be on record. Birth dates. Death dates. Marriage dates. Affinity Age. Amount of magical blood: full, half, quarter.

And I wasn't on any records yet.

My affinity hadn't settled into anything useful yet—the curse of the quarter mage—and if it did, my mother was determined to prove it was fire magic rather than the *other* magic I might have inherited: mind magic. If I manifested that affinity, I'd be tossed in the Labyrinth before I could say *fates forbid.*

So, it was burn to death or be thrown in a prison designed to drive me mad. One would at least be quicker.

My legs throttled on toward home while my mind entertained the possibility of running away. But with every hurried step, I couldn't bring myself to deviate from the well-known roads that would take me to our cottage, where I would don this wedding gown and cart off to the temple to either get married or die. A crackling sliver of hope, as blatant and alluring as a candle in a dark room, the one that told me I'd survive and that I'd finally find my place in this world, pushed me onward...a hope that said, what if, despite all the evidence to the contrary, I actually *was* a fire mage?

A few minutes later, I blasted through our front door, and my mother tossed a disgusted look toward my dirty hem—or perhaps her scrutiny was intended for all of me. My brothers, Archer and Danny, were still asleep in the bed tucked into the far corner, but my loud entrance woke them.

"Out, out!" my mother barked, shooing them toward the door. "Vera must get dressed, and it's bad luck for a man to be in the building."

Groggily, my two younger brothers stumbled into the small garden behind our front wall. Archer shot me an *I'll get you later* look and shook his head, his long blond hair swishing over his shoulders. Danny squatted down on his ankles and began picking at the weeds between the lettuce and the flowers. Mother shut the door, a little too forcefully, and practically dove for the parcel containing my wedding dress.

"Did anyone see you?"

"No, Mother."

Her hiss of relief seared my already frazzled nerves.

An hour later, my mother tossed a heavy black cloak over my shoulders, concealing the dull gray lace beneath. She stepped away quickly, but not so fast that I missed the cringe on her tired face.

I pursed my lips. "I will not light you on fire on the way to the temple." *Though if I did, at least it would prove I'm your precious fire mage.* The thought weighed heavy in my stomach.

She looked me up and down. "Keep the cloak wrapped tight as we exit the carriage. No one can see you. No one can know a fire mage wedding is taking place."

"Until it's over, and I'm still alive, and you can finally celebrate my burdensome existence."

My mother pinched her thin lips, for once not retaliating. She was, if possible, more nervous than I was today, the day our family would—once and for all—learn which quarter of magical blood truly ran in my veins. Of course, it wasn't her head that would have a flaming ring of fire placed on it.

But I wouldn't think about that now. My eyes rolled from one end of our tiny sitting room to the other. Thin curls of candle smoke lifted to the soot-stained ceiling, infusing the room with the faint honey scent of beeswax. The flickering flame danced, impressing me with its loveliness, a cruel reminder that fire could both heal and hurt, light and destroy. A shudder crawled down my spine as I tried to make the flame stand straight. It was the simplest of the fire mage tests...and one I'd failed enough times to know this magic wasn't in my blood. But I'd also *passed* twice—forcing a flame to stand erect and still as a sculpture—just enough to call into question my entire definition of myself. Enough to convince my mother that I would be a good wife for a fully trained, fully terrifying fire mage.

This would be the last time I set foot in this house, the house that had raised me. I'd known this day would come, and yet it grated on me, a bit like the scratchy wool of my school dress.

For everyone else, weddings were a cause for celebration, occasions to be marked with friends, flowers, and fine food. My wedding, however, was a secret—unannounced, unadorned, and unaccompanied by food of any kind.

I met my mother's eyes, but she looked quickly away. Was that a twinge of regret? Or sadness? Surely not. I tried to parcel out what well-guarded emotions might swim in her depths, as this might be my final opportunity to do so. If I could but pull one tear from her eye on this day of our parting, would it satisfy me?

"Mother," I said, my own throat stupidly thick. I tried to shove my emotions into the box I usually kept them in, but they were misbehaving today.

"You must not look at anyone on the street, or any temple staff not involved in the ceremony. Until it is over, that is, and you are..."

"No longer your problem." *No longer alive* threatened to squeak out of my clamped throat, but my voice failed and I couldn't say it.

She cut flat eyes at me that warned of provoking her. "You are marrying a man capable of handling you. You will never be anyone's problem again."

I angled my chin to the side as if slapped. She always did have the best way of compiling sentences, stacking up words like perfect little hammer strokes to my wellbeing. Eighteen years of hammering me into the earth. Today, for her at least, would be the final nailing of the coffin.

The giving away of her quarter-mage daughter.

The room screamed memories at me: wrestling my brothers, completing schoolwork, sitting in front of the fire, wishing I had the guts to stick my hands into the flames and make the fire obey me.

So rare was my magic's appearance that in eighteen long years, we had still never witnessed its true manifestation. All the full and half-mages would be graduating next year, and I'd be making babies for some fire lord who only needed a vehicle for his powerful children to enter the world. A vehicle that wouldn't protest, as my mother assured me I was not to do.

I tugged my eyes from the worn lattice chairs by the window. Archer, with his incessant bouncing, had busted both seats so many times that we'd positioned the biggest books we owned across the frame rather than paying to repair the lattice again. The emptiness of the chairs struck me as a solemn thing, almost like a pair of gravestones. No more evenings crammed beside my younger brother, finishing lessons until the light of day faded into starlight.

Danny, who'd always had to sit on the floor, would take my place in the chair on the right. That was good. But it still hurt.

In a final, desperate attempt to save my own life, I walked over to the burning candles and stretched my palm out over a flickering flame.

"Vera, what are you doing?" my mother snapped.

"I'm not a fire mage, no matter how convenient that would be for you." *And for me.*

Her eyes danced between my hand and my face.

My skin smarted from the heat. I jerked my hand away. "See? The fire burns me too."

Being able to light candles from across a room was *not* evidence that I was a burner—the other term for fire mages. Every affinity had a title, like architect or burner or, in the case of mind mages, meddler—though I was fairly certain they'd gone by a different name before the war. Some people went as far as calling mind mages vampires, as they fed on the minds of other people. I'd been teased with enough vampire jokes at school to heartily prefer the term meddler to anything else. Though I'd never once shown any signs of having the affinity for mind magic, that was the only other type of magic in my heritage, and mages could only manifest *one* kind of magic.

"Curse the king's canaries, Vera," she hissed. "Your grandfather was a fire mage. It *is* in your blood. We're not going through this again. A wealthy man has agreed to marry you, which is more than we could have ever wished for."

"It's exactly what you've always wished for." I kept wide, unfeeling eyes on her. My blood was certainly more my maternal grandmother's than my mother's or even my father's, as evidenced by my dark hair, rounded nose, deep set eyes, and stork legs. My mother took after her father, the fire mage, in all but magic. Stocky, blonde, and sharp as icicles.

"And he knows what Nan was, doesn't he? You promised you would tell him."

My mother, her long hair piled on top of her head, turned toward the door to our cottage. "We are leaving."

"You didn't tell him."

"It won't matter once you're married." She shrugged and pulled on a traveling cloak from the peg by the back door. Her cloak had been scrubbed of all stains, at least the removable ones. She looked presentable, if a little worn around the eyes, as she sighed and reached for the door.

It was the law to divulge all magical heritage to one's betrothed. Before the wedding. But in our case, we'd hung every hope on the fact that affinity would turn out to be fire magic. If we were wrong, I'd be dead anyway.

She yanked open the door and stepped into the bright sunlight. Outside, my brothers' voices launched into so many questions at once that I couldn't catch a single one.

A wave of panic swept over me. Dead. Burned. Finished. Like punches from my brother, the thoughts pelted my mind. My hand still stung from where I'd held it over the fire a moment ago. I stared at the flame across the room, anger blazing in my chest. *Stand still*, I commanded it silently.

The flame reached higher, freezing for a single heartbeat. I gasped, but the flame went back to flickering merrily.

Archer popped his head in the doorway, his long hair swishing past his face. "You are *finally* ready? What were you doing in here so long?"

"Putting on a lace wedding dress." I lifted my arms and the cloak parted slightly. "I hooked my thumbs in the silly sleeves six times." I attempted to put out the candles with another silent command, but nothing happened. I marched to the candles and blew them out.

He quirked an eyebrow and stumbled forward into the room. "You're really leaving us."

My arms fell back to my sides. Tears immediately welled up. I wanted to quash them, but they dumped over my cheeks and poured off my chin.

"I'll still see you."

"When?" He snorted. His beliefs about my magic were as ill-founded as my mother's, but somehow, the hope in his voice that suggested I would survive this wedding and actually be too busy as a wife and mother to see my own brothers brought a smile to my face that temporarily loosened the invisible gallows noose around my throat.

"I won't miss your graduation," I said.

He glanced at the floor. "That's in two years."

"Then I'll come to your recitals."

"Mother might not…"

I stormed forward. "Oh, she will let you continue learning piano or I will burn this house down."

His eyes widened.

"Not really, Arch."

"Oh, right."

After a quick shove in the shoulder, I pulled him into a tight hug. He hugged back. It was the first time we'd really hugged in…a long time. Since we'd stopped pretending to ride the broom like it was a horse.

His arms loosened, and we stepped apart, awkwardly clearing our throats and wiping away tears. Archer was already taller than me.

"Stop growing, or Mother might think you have grandmother's blood in there somewhere."

His smile faltered. "Da was tall."

"Arch, you do realize that even if you turn out to have some sliver of Nan's blood, you'll still be the same person?"

Archer and Danny had never shown any signs of having magic, to my mother's great delight. At nine, it wasn't unheard of that Danny might still manifest an affinity, but he'd never shown a single early sign of possessing magic. But Archer, at sixteen, was quickly aging out. The oldest documented age of an affinity showing up was seventeen, but that was rare, and Archer had never experienced any strange bursts of magical ability, the way I did. No, Mother only had to worry about *one* of her children turning out to have her mother-in-law's wicked mind magic.

"What if *you* turn out to have her magic?" Archer asked.

I moved like I was about to shove my elbow into his stomach. He braced with his palms out to block me and then chuckled.

"Then I'll die today when that ring of fire descends onto my head."

Archer's bright face collapsed into a tight frown. "Don't say that."

Outside, Danny yelled from the carriage to hurry up. With a sigh, I walked past Archer toward the still open door.

"Such is life for the Mystery Quarter," I muttered, using one of the nicknames my schoolmates had thrown at me over the years. Quarter mages were rare; magic usually manifested powerfully, both in full-blooded mages and in half-mages. For magic to be fitful, passive, and unidentifiable by the Guilds was like having an incurable illness, and people feared it would contaminate them should they get too near. Being magicless was far superior to being *occasionally* magical.

"Ver."

I spun back to face my brother. He seemed entirely too old in that moment.

"If I'm not a fire mage, then we all know what I am," I muttered.

My brother's face paled, and it looked like a boy's face again despite his stature. "You are a fire mage. So what if your magic is spotty? You're a quarter, not a full." He hesitated, then added, "You don't have to marry him."

I wanted him to be right about my magic, that it would come through for me on the day I needed it most. I didn't want to die today, and though I could acknowledge that I *might* die, I could no more believe that I would than I could believe my arms were wings.

I nodded, trying to encourage him, but my stomach felt hollow as the next words fell from my mouth. "It's just the next prison, Arch. It won't be that different."

Before he could reply, I stepped outside into the blinding sunlight.

2

Danny, crammed on the wagon seat between Archer and Mother, squirmed so much that he popped off the seat. He quickly slithered onto Mother's lap.

"You're too heavy," she protested, wrapping both arms around his middle.

At their displays of affection, I felt both warm and empty, somewhat like a teakettle freshly divested of its contents. He ate up her affection, as any son would, and his smile always made me smile in return. It also showed me something I'd never known and would never know.

Archer, of late grown too observant for a young man, cleared his throat in that pointed way he did when he saw something in the world he thought was unjust. Mother, of course, missed it entirely. A lawman could hand her a notice with her crimes emblazoned on it and she would accept it with a smile and a nod and complete dismissal. Willing blindness was her strongest attribute.

The wagon jostled our shoulders and knees together.

"My, the king must send his architects soon, or this road will wash clean into the Imperial Forest," Mother commented as she nearly toppled sideways with Danny.

Our family wagon trundled along the twin grooves in the path toward the high town—the king's town. It wasn't far, but the road between Varich to Westburg encountered heavy rains this time of year and was in serious need of a Guild architect—someone with constructive magic—to come and smooth things over.

"The architects don't come until the end of summer," I said. "As always," I added under my breath at my mother's sniff of disapproval. In the kingdom of Bevon, the Guilds were nearly worshipped for the help they could give to our society. The problem was, they didn't give their help unless the king expressly allowed it, thanks in part to his fear of anyone being praised but himself.

Up ahead, the bridge that marked Silver Creek rolled into view.

Danny scrambled to put his feet in Mother's lap, but he didn't fit anymore. Archer scoffed and rolled his eyes. Danny might be too old to sit in Mother's lap, but Mother still thought of him as her little boy, and her affection for him had only grown steadily stronger since an illness three years ago had nearly taken him.

"Nothing's going to crawl out of the water and eat you," Archer said, jabbing Danny with an elbow.

Danny stiffened, then slowly let his legs back down. Tears welled up in his brown eyes.

"You're crying. Again." Archer heaved a sigh and looked at me, shaking his head.

I shot him a look of silent reproof. Danny had been scared of Silver Creek for years, and it was all Archer's fault. Every time we crossed this bridge, his childhood fears resurfaced, the clock seemed to rewind, and Danny turned back into a four-year-old boy.

A boy who didn't know how to swim.

A boy who believed every fairy tale he'd ever heard.

When Archer had pushed Danny into the creek, telling him the Labyrinth monsters swam through its shallow depths and feasted on lost boys, it had cemented in my youngest brother a perpetual fear of all water.

After that, I'd never let Danny go with Archer into the Imperial Forest—the home of the Labyrinth and Silver Creek. I'd stayed with them. Always. Until now. Now I was leaving them.

I stared at Archer. He'd grown taller, but that didn't mean he was ready to take care of Danny in all the ways Danny needed. Archer read my expression and rolled his eyes. He chewed his lower lip, peering down at the creek as it rolled underneath us, as if to say, *Look, I'm not teasing him now.*

The glittering water appeared innocent, almost happy, burbling along its merry way. But it flowed from the Labyrinth, and its waters provided fodder for myths and nightmares alike. No one drew water from this creek, and farmers refused to let their animals drink from its cool pools. This was cursed water, touched by the madness of the Labyrinth, a prison crafted to contain history's most wicked mage, the one who nearly tore the kingdom apart in his attempt to take the throne for his own. He'd craved power and stolen it with his mind, showing the world what mind magic was truly capable of.

Despite his bravado, Archer turned his head to watch the creek disappear from view behind us as the road curved. He caught me watching him.

"I mean, how does *it* flow out, but nothing else can?" Archer shook his head, launching into his favorite topic. "If the water can get out, the things inside should also be able to. It doesn't make sense."

"It was built by magic," I countered, which dismissed the Labyrinth from obeying logic or natural laws.

"It isn't safe," Danny added.

Archer bumped his brother's shoulder. "The monsters can swim out. They do it every night."

"You just said nothing else can get out!" Danny shoved him back.

"Stop it, you two." I grabbed Danny's hands before he could claw at Archer's face.

"Not the eyes! Fates, Dan!" Archer shoved us both off.

Meanwhile, Mother sat silent, watching the forest roll by as if she were alone in this trundling carriage.

Danny tucked his hands between his legs and hung his head low. Shame, surging up like the geysers down in the valley, always followed when Archer used that tone with him.

Forced to employ only silent communication, I pinned a scowl on Archer. But he ignored me, already reaching an arm around Danny's shoulders and tilting his body so that he could rub his knuckles into his brother's hair.

Mother yelped slightly as Danny jostled out of her lap and settled beside Archer.

Maybe things would turn out okay. Maybe Archer was ready to be the brother Danny needed. I couldn't very well worry about it now, considering I quite possibly would never see Danny or Archer ever again.

But that thought brought a sudden wave of tears, so I shoved my sadness away and turned my thoughts back to Silver Creek. Flowing directly from the Labyrinth, its origins were hidden within the walls of the prison. The creek, according to legend, hadn't been there when the Labyrinth was constructed. Now, its waters slithered through our woods, bearing, as rumor had it, the remains of the bodies that died in the Labyrinth. The architects could do nothing about this creek. Not divert it. Not dam it. No amount of magic could affect that water.

But the worst part was, all the children in Varich believed that if the water could get out, *something else* could theoretically get out too. And the only things in the Labyrinth were the kingdom's worst criminals and untold monsters.

When the sun was directly overhead, our wagon pulled up to a pointed little temple less than a block away from the grand temple, the massive building where the king worshipped. I was not to be wed there, of course.

The horse hung his head, weary from carting all four of us up the incline into Westburg. These cobbled roads had left my teeth rattling and my pulse clanging in my temples.

"Here we are," my mother announced, scrambling from the wagon like she couldn't wait to proceed with the ceremony. She quite possibly could lose her daughter, but that apparently didn't bother her.

Archer, who'd extended his hand to help Mother, glanced back at me. The boy was entirely too observant. Much more so than the ignorant boys at school, who, though two years older than Archer, hardly noticed when a girl was without a seat and had to stand in the back of the classroom. Danny leaped off the wagon, fell rather dramatically to his knees, and immediately tore a hole in his nicest pair of pants.

Mother gasped.

Danny's brown eyes welled with unshed tears.

Archer rolled his eyes, but he patted Danny on the back, staring at me over our brother's shoulders.

Our family was a mess. And I was leaving them.

Glancing up at the green-tinted steeple, I huffed in annoyance at whoever it might be pointing to. Years ago, the king had decreed every house of worship devoted to the magical affinities be converted to a temple of the fates, celestial beings that apparently ruled us like chess pieces. As if we were part of some divine game.

Archer hurried a distraught Danny inside, not bothering to wait for Mother or me. I hated to see them go, but this was good. Archer would be taking over. I could no longer protect Danny, and it did my soul good to see Archer acting like he knew it too.

This, however, left me standing beside my mother outside what had once been a temple of fire. Odd that the king, with his demand for steeples and statues, didn't also decree the bronze doors ripped from their hinges. Depicted on the tall doors were figures standing in flames. Fire mages.

"Well, come along," she said. "And remember, you must not say a word until the ceremony is over, you hear?" Her blue eyes flared.

Clutching the cloak more tightly around my middle, I did my best to stare blankly at the temple doors beyond her head. "If I don't say the vows, we won't technically be married."

She barked in frustration and whirled toward the steps, storming forward in a tumult of fluttering fabric. Where she'd procured her dress or the money for it, I had no idea.

I paused beside the heavy bronze doors. The temples dotting this city marked a time long past, a time when the people worshipped those with magic. The figures etched in flame sent a chill down my spine. The test for fire mages used to require passing through flame. At least the test had changed, and I hadn't been sent through fire as a child to test my affinity.

This building, with its rounded arches and flaming capitals atop its columns, was constructed long before the war, before schools were built to teach mages from the Guilds how to hone their magic. Mind magic, like Nan's, was forbidden after the war, and for good reason. It had been the reason for the war and caused the deaths of thousands.

I passed through the smaller door that had been set into the larger one on the right. Those ancient doors stood like headstones marking the grave of an entire worldview.

The cool air of the church chilled my face, but my cloak kept the summer heat clinging to my body. I blinked in the dim light, searching for Archer and Danny...then for my mother. I couldn't see a single person in this vaulted space.

My mother had only just entered.

"Hello?" My voice echoed off the stone walls, traipsed down the nave, and then bounced back to me, as if the temple was saying hello back. Alcoves on both sides featured defaced statues, naked except for the writhing flames curling up legs and torsos. The air smelled fragile and damp.

"There you are."

A woman hurried forward.

I jumped at her sudden arrival, blinking and unsure how to respond.

"Come, come, they're all back here."

The woman, large and overly adorned with jewels, jangled down the long nave, her arms waving like a scarecrow's. "I'm to show you to the chamber where you'll await the ceremony."

I spotted the dark ring tattooed around her wrists and the black diamonds tattooed beside her ears: marks of a mage who'd chosen to become a slave of the king, bound by enchantments to do his bidding.

The cold air in the vaulted space sliced through the remaining heat on my skin and I shivered. Or maybe it was just this woman's presence.

She shot me a cunning look, as if aware of the way her presence affected me.

My heart rate quadrupled, and the fear I'd wrestled into submission this morning came bursting out again. I might die before the next bell chimed the hour. Desperate for a delay, for any reason not to follow this woman, I asked, "Can you tell me the name of the man I am to marry?"

Instead of answering, she shooed me away from the front doors, off to a side chapel crammed with a golden box and about a hundred lit candles. Above the candles, engraved on the wall, was a picture of the king, a man who, despite his youthful appearance, was older than anyone else living. His crown glowed in the candlelight.

I was no longer certain who or what this temple was meant to honor.

The woman opened a door, shoving me through it and into a narrow, tiled hallway. She then led me to a small chamber with yet another altar. It was almost cozy in here with a small rug, a single painting, and the warm glow of six candles.

But upon closer inspection, this room fed me an eerie chill.

The rug was threadbare in two small places right before the altar, presumably from someone kneeling. The candlelight flickered off mostly bare stone walls that reminded me of the flames outside the Westburg prison.

A single ring of metal, large enough to fit my head, lay on the altar.

My heart rattled against my ribs like a panicked animal.

"Wait here, dear."

The woman shoved my shoulder, and I stumbled toward the altar. One of my mother's too-large slippers stayed on the floor behind me. She'd insisted I wear them. They were nicer than my everyday shoes.

"Where's Archer?"

The woman merely lifted her brows and backed out of the room, shutting the door behind her.

Trembling, I scooted my foot into the lost slipper and backed away from the altar. When a fire mage graduated from the academy, their final test was to ignite a ring of metal and place it on their wrist. This was how they proved their learning, their mastery. The fire mage wedding ceremony featured the man igniting a ring of metal, then placing it on his bride's head.

I'd never seen one of these placed on the head or wrist of someone *not* immune to flame.

My hands reached up to touch my hair. A quick glance showed me this was more like a prison cell than a bridal room for wedding ceremonies. No furniture, save the altar, and nothing soft, save the threadbare rug.

Mother had always harbored hope that I'd have enough fire mage blood in me to make me useful to the Guild, but attempting to force me to do magic I couldn't do wouldn't grant her wish. Panic rising, I leaned against the wall, the fabric of my cloak sticking to the rough, cool stones.

The door swung open, and a man stepped inside, followed by the large woman who'd led me here, and finally, my mother.

The man wore a black robe trimmed with red, the ceremonial attire for male fire mages. His top hat boasted a red band and the unmistakable emblem of a fire mage: a split flame with a ring around it. The way he moved and the way the red underside of his cloak flashed in and out of view gave him a sinister look—like some wicked circus master who had come to claim me.

His face was lined and his beard peppered with gray. He was handsome in a way, but I nearly gagged.

After appraising me for a single breath, he walked toward the altar, grabbed the iron ring, and swung it toward me, holding it out at arm's length.

"Light it on fire, and I will marry you."

My eyes bulged as I realized the moment had come.

3

My mother nodded firmly, a warning look in her eyes, then tossed a nervous glance at the woman who'd entered behind my groom. The mage squared her shoulders and clasped her hands in front of her ample waist, chin lifted like she was watching a student evaluation. A jolt shook me. She was sent here by the Guild. They'd found out I was getting married after all, a quarter mage with *either* mind or fire magic, and they'd sent a witness.

My mouth opened and my eyes fixed on the metal ring. Usually, the man lit it on fire first.

No words came out, no sound, only a wisp of breath. I'd meant to say a proper goodbye to Archer and Danny. I swallowed. I'd assumed they'd be here to watch, but I could see why they weren't. In case things...ended poorly.

The fire mage looked back at my mother. "She can do this, yes? I paid for a woman who can bear children for me. I'm not making the same mistake again."

Thoughts tumbled through my muddled brain. *Paid for. Same mistake.* My eyes locked on my mother, who was staring pointedly at the altar.

The hole that existed inside me, the one I patched over with smiles from Danny and jokes from Archer, with reading and wildflowers and the smell of fresh herbs or the warmth of sunshine on a crisp morning, tore open, and every hope I'd harbored that my mother would choose today to reveal her well-hidden love for me crashed to the stone floor.

I pressed my hands against my middle and willed the ache inside me to dissolve.

"Well?" the mage barked, shaking the ring at me.

A dog, purchased to breed little fire-wreathed pups for this man, that's what I was. My mother had sold me.

Sold me.

I stared at the outstretched ring, seeking to find the heat in the atmosphere that I could call down as fire—as the training had indicated. Fire mages could manipulate heat in precise ways, but only if they could feel it. I felt nothing but the damp air of the small room.

The man huffed and turned toward my mother and the woman hovering close behind him. "She can't, can she?"

I wasn't sure which hurt worse: the disappointment on my mother's face or the knowledge that I couldn't do the one thing that would give me a place in society. I cleared my throat, drawing the man's attention once more.

With every ounce of my concentration, I screamed inside my head for the stupid ring to catch fire.

Nothing.

If he lit it on fire, I'd feel those flames catching in my hair and then the end would come. I couldn't do it. In a single breath, my hope died and I spewed out the one thing that I could think of that would be my ticket out of this room.

"My grandmother was a—"

"Hush your mouth," Mother snapped.

"—mind mage," I finished over my mother's reprimand.

The man's lined face curled into a feral snarl. "A what?"

Fabric rustled and the other woman stepped forward. "If this woman is a mind mage, it's possible she manipulated her mother, and you, sir, into this deal."

My jaw fell open, and I lifted my shoulders to my full height, which was still shorter than everyone else in the room. "I am a *quarter mage*. I don't have enough control for something like that. I don't even know if I *have* mind magic." My pulse trilled in my ears and my heart felt like it was throwing punches against my ribs.

"She's using it on us now, to make us believe her," the woman said.

An angry scream tore from my lips. My mother's eyes grew wide and burned with sharp reproof. I lunged for the door, feeling trapped in this tiny space, but the large woman blocked my exit.

A flame flickered before my face, and I stopped cold, terrified by how close the fire ring hovered before my nose. It didn't smell like normal fire with its comforting wood-smoke aroma. This fire smelled acrid, like it was stealing something for fuel that was not supposed to burn.

"You will cease your magic and tell me the truth," the man said as he held out the flaming ring. "Are you capable of bearing my children?"

A shudder coursed through me. Keeping my eyes on the flame, I spoke through gritted teeth. "I am no fire mage."

The flame flickered out, and a breath escaped my lungs.

"Then I have no need of you."

The moment I stepped toward the door, the woman's hand grabbed my arm—hard.

"If you are not a fire mage, then the only other magic in you is illegal."

Cold fear lanced through my veins, mixing with hot anger.

A quick gasp from my mother stole the single moment I had to escape. As I took my next breath, something strange descended over me—a feeling of ease, to the point of stupor. I was unable to remember why I wanted so badly to walk out the narrow wooden door, although a part of my mind was aware that I should leave.

The fire mage, whose name I still didn't know, stormed out of the room demanding his money back. My mother clasped a hand over her mouth and slumped against the stone wall, deflated. I'd never seen her look so disappointed in her life.

"Listen carefully." The woman still holding my arm spoke with a firm, quiet voice. "You will follow me. We are going to walk out that door, get in my carriage, and travel far away from here."

I blinked. My mind suddenly felt a tug, as if a fisherman had dropped a hook at my brain and my brain had bitten.

She was a mind mage. And I'd just taken the bait.

Groaning, I stepped after her, no more able to deny her commands than a fish could save itself from a hook through the gills.

As we entered the hallway, my gaze swept past my mother, who stood watching me like I'd transformed into a monster from the Labyrinth. She was trembling, but her pinched lips showed more rage than fright. Even now, as this mage was bending my body to her will, my mother looked on, angry that I'd let her down. If my muscles had been under my command, I might have screamed or wilted under the sudden flood of hopelessness that swept through me. But I kept marching after the mind mage, unable to resist. My eyes roved the hall, hoping for a glimpse of Archer peeking through a doorway, his hands reaching for me or his voice calling for me.

But no one was coming to save me.

My legs stepped stiffly after the mage, testifying to the awful power of mind magic. I'd never been under someone else's control like this; now, I fully agreed that this kind of magic *should* be illegal. My blood boiled in defiance, but that was the only part of me to resist. My arms and legs simply kept moving. My intentions were fragile as eggshells, and they cracked as soon as they contradicted my captor's will.

I tested my voice, but even my throat and tongue were under this woman's control. A low growl was all that escaped.

My mother's presence hovered behind me, but I couldn't turn to her. She wasn't objecting to this.

At a door cut into the external wall of the temple, the mage paused and looked back at me, then my mother. "The crime of concealing one's magical affinity is severe, and the Guild will not tolerate it."

My mother emitted some garbled, trembling sound. I still could not turn to see her face. Being imprisoned in my own flesh was maddening. Sweat leaked into my lace wedding dress.

"You've been clever to conceal your magic," she said to me, "but we've been watching you for years, and now we know for certain you're not a fire mage. This ceremony proved what we never could."

My eyes narrowed into slits and my heavy breathing quickened. To my shock, my mother's cold hand descended onto my exposed shoulder, a ghoulish touch against my hot skin. Out of the corner of my eye, I saw her nod.

"She's only a quarter," my mother said, reminding me of my lack yet again.

"Quarter mage or not, she'll come with me. King's orders."

Where are we going? screamed in my head, but my mouth didn't work.

Then the mage nodded at my mother with a finality that terrified me. She was taking me away, and that nod meant we weren't coming back. Rebellion surged up inside me, battering against the woman's control on my mind.

"No!" I managed a single word. Then the control on my brain latched down tighter, my throat closing up so violently that I wheezed when I tried to draw breath.

My mother lifted her hand from my shoulder to cover her mouth once again. She looked pale as wax but said nothing as my body lurched through the door after the mage.

I followed the mind mage out a squat back door into summer sunlight that didn't quite reach the alley floor. The shadows were deep here. My limbs were on marionette strings, moving in slow, jerkish movements that signaled to anyone watching that I was not acting of my own accord. Unfortunately, no one was watching.

I narrowed my eyes at my captor; at least my eyes were still under my own command. This woman had accused me of being a mind mage, when she was one herself.

Mind magic had been outlawed the moment the war had ended, almost eighty years ago. There would be no more schools for mind mages, no lessons exploring its depths and dangers or uses and possibilities. Those caught using it faced a lifetime in the king's inescapable prison.

But it appeared the king still liked to employ a few mind mages, for times like this. Dragging people away was much easier when they couldn't resist.

The woman led me to a waiting carriage, its door already open, and practically shoved my rear end inside. I flopped into the seat, the heavy lace dress adding to the stifling feeling inside this enclosed black box. Sweat soaked into my would-be wedding dress.

The large woman shook the carriage as she took her seat across from me, a satisfied smile curling the edges of her painted lips.

"Excellent. You've done well." She fiddled with her skirt, smoothing it and adjusting the folds beneath her.

I wanted to scream, to beat my fists against the windows. Instead, my hands remained clasped compliantly in my lap. The only thing indicating my distress was my thundering pulse.

She knocked on the wall of the coach, and we rolled away from the temple...and from my family.

I tried once more to speak, but nothing happened. I understood now, better than from any lesson in a history book, why some people assumed the magic wielders were gods, toying with us. A flash of clarity jolted through me. My mother's hatred of what I might be suddenly made more sense, though it still didn't excuse her behavior.

As we bumped across the cobblestones, I nearly fell over in the seat several times, until the woman relaxed her hold on my muscles enough that I could balance.

I tried to reach for the door.

"Not so fast," my captor cooed.

My arm remained pinned at my side. My glare hardened, and the sweat intensified as my anger deepened. This woman could control certain muscles in my body while relaxing others. It was a level of control I'd never dreamed was possible.

Nan had lived through the war, seen the atrocities mind magic had performed. She'd been young, one of the last mind mages to receive official training. She never complained when her magic was outlawed, never complained when the king literally burned every temple and toppled every statue dedicated to her affinity. She always said it was for the best, always complied with every regulation, every new law restricting her magic. She'd passed away before the regulations had intensified and the king had decreed that every mind mage was to be thrown into the Labyrinth.

My Nan had only ever performed mind magic in front of me once. It was the day Grandpa died. When my mother found him face down in the garden, she nearly lost herself with grief. She'd had a sharp trowel in her hand, and I'd been attempting to take it from her madly flailing hands. Nan had stilled my mother's movements and loosened her grip on the metal blade.

No one had reported Nan's use of magic, but she'd felt burdened to do so. Watching Nan walk through the streets, her wrists in iron shackles, had pinched my heart with an ache that never really let go. She was too old and frail for such humiliation. My family never recovered from the incessant snide remarks, both about Nan and about my mother; the details of why Nan had used her magic had been publicly announced by the magistrate as he'd manacled her in the town square.

My eyes drifted to the woman. She was clearly well-educated in forbidden magic. I'd heard rumors of secret Guilds, underground academies for mind magic. Archer had teased me about running off with these secret mind mage Guilds every time I came home late from the market or after wandering too long in the meadows by our house.

But in my entire life, I'd never *made anyone do something.* There had never been proof that I had Nan's magic—in fact, there was more proof that I had Grandpa's magic, spotty as the evidence was.

I couldn't lift my arms or legs, but when I tried again, I loosed my tongue from the roof of my mouth.

"Where are you taking me?"

The woman *tsked* at me. "You should have asked a better question—"

My tongue once again froze in my mouth.

"—while you had the chance." She flashed a mirthless grin. "You will *see* where we're going when we get there." Her shoulders shifted back and forth in a satisfied way.

The carriage soon rolled from cobblestones to dirt road and passed the last buildings at the edge of Westburg, their outline through the lace carriage curtains fading into the dull green and brown of the Imperial Forest.

She was going to dump me in the Labyrinth without a trial.

I'd never even performed mind magic and likely couldn't pass the tests they'd put me through at the Guild. I never thought I'd *want* to go to the Guild for the mind mage probes, but everything inside me burned with fury at the thought of being denied this right.

I tried to make my eyes say what my tongue couldn't.

The woman chuckled at my scowl but pressed two fingers to her lips. Sweat beaded on her brow, and I sensed it was not merely from the heat.

Holding me captive like this was draining her.

If only I knew how to use mind magic, I might be able to resist her, to break free of her mental hold. But my magic was finicky, and even if I had learned all the mysterious ways of mind mages—of meddlers—my powers always slipped from my fingers right at the moment I needed them most.

After several more silent minutes during which I glared at her and she ignored me, the carriage slowed to a stop. My heart lurched. We were deep in the forest.

Like an actor following stage directions, I moved toward the door, unlatching the handle and stepping out into deep shadows. Stumbling off the carriage step, I fell to the ground in a part of the forest so thick that very little sunlight reached me.

I glanced back at the woman in the carriage. She waggled her fingers and flashed a sinister smile.

Her magic compelled me forward. My foot hooked a root, and I went down again. For the briefest moment, I felt my mind return and my limbs flood with tingling energy. I scrambled to my feet and turned, only to find the movement excruciating.

I groaned and turned back the way the woman wanted me to go, toward a single, free-standing blue door half-covered in vines that hadn't been there a moment ago. The paint on the door had cracked and worn off, showing the dull brown wood beneath. I knew this door. Every child in Westburg and Varich had heard tales of this door.

The door that populated infinite myths and nightmares.

A scream tore from my bespelled lips, overriding the magic that controlled my movements for a single, earsplitting exhale.

This was the door to the Labyrinth.

For the first time in my life, I wanted nothing more than to possess my grandmother's power. I tried to remember what I'd heard other mages say.

Concentrate.

Keep your eyes open.

Feel it in your bones.

Draw it from your blood.

I'd heard mages talk about their magic—they all seemed keen to do so around those of us who couldn't perform such wonders—but I'd never understood what it meant to *draw it from your blood*. My blood was hot and racing, but it didn't feel laced with power.

My feet mercilessly marched toward the door. She would force me to open it, force me to enter. And I could do nothing to stop it. I would be lost forever.

My mind churned. A growl rose from low in my throat. Every step was labored as I fought to resist her magic. Physical strength was part of this game. If I could just push hard enough, I could break her magic. She was already tired, after all.

With every ounce of my energy, I ground my heel into the leaf-strewn earth. My muscles trembled. Words I wanted to shout bottled up in my mouth and throat.

The Labyrinth door loomed ahead of me. It stood without walls, and no prison was visible behind it. The Labyrinth's walls were part of the mystery—they were entirely invisible, leaving us to wonder if the magic that held the great prison together had broken, and all the monsters had burst into our world. But King Geoffrey assured his people that the Labyrinth was unbreakable, maintained by the king of the beasts, a monster created by the Labyrinth for the Labyrinth.

A monster whose sole aim was to tear to pieces the sanity of those tossed into the maze.

My feet drew near to the door. My hands shook.

Archer's face swam before me. Danny's smile. Our little sitting room, with a fire in the grate. Mother humming as she patched one of Danny's pant legs again. I would never see them again if my feet crossed that threshold.

Only madness waited within.

"Why?" A single word croaked from my pinched throat. I could hardly do magic at all, and I had never performed mind magic in my life.

The woman's voice shook slightly, as if strained from the effort, as she answered from behind me. "You conspired to hide your affinity from the king. If it was discovered that your affinity was meddling—as it was today—I had my orders from the king to bring you here. As I brought your grandmother and will likely bring your brothers, should they manifest any signs of magic."

My heart sank so deeply that I tried to clutch my aching chest, but my arms didn't move. My brothers. The king was watching them too.

"In fact," the woman called out as I stumbled toward the Labyrinth door, "you can ask your grandmother all about it. That is, if she's not dead already."

Nan was in the Labyrinth? I'd attended her *funeral*. My head whirled around, and rage exploded. "Fates curse the king!"

The woman's eyes widened, and the hold on my muscles tightened. But I wasn't taking this anymore. Like opening a heavy door, I pushed with all my strength against the magic controlling me. Eyes watering from the effort, I took one slow step toward my captor.

She barreled toward me, anger distorting her features.

A prickling sensation snagged my ankles and wrists, and the burn against my skin grew unbearable. A faint hissing sound accompanied my yelps of pain.

"You're not what you think you are, little quarter. And it's better if you never found out."

With that, a force like a boot to my stomach sent me pinwheeling backward. My shoulders slammed into the wooden door, and my head ricocheted forward. My mind fuzzed, and my resistance to her magic fell away.

The door gave way behind me, and I fell into the Labyrinth.

4

The first sensation was blind panic.

The second was the wind being knocked from my lungs as I landed on my back.

Momentarily dazed, I writhed on the ground, slinging leaves and snagging even more on my lace dress. All the myths, all the fears, and all the nasty stories children concocted to scare each other flooded my mind and numbed my awareness.

I scrambled to my feet and took in my prison.

I could see no walls, which made it so much worse. A prison without walls tricked the mind, making it feel like escape was possible. But the most powerful mages in the world couldn't escape this place. And I'd just been locked in—before I could even tell my family goodbye.

A hollow ache gnawed at my insides, and I bent forward, clutching my stomach and gasping as my brothers' names fell from my lips.

The woman had been clear—if Danny or Archer showed any signs of magic, they'd land in here too. Dazed by a whirlwind of thoughts, I fleetingly wondered what she'd meant when she said I wasn't what I thought I was.

Maybe Archer wasn't what we thought he was either. Maybe he'd manifest magic next month and they'd toss him in here. Would I even still be alive in a month?

My flood of thoughts ceased as if it had crashed into a solid wall. A single, overwhelming thought remained.

Yes.

Yes, I would still be alive in a month.

My fingers curled into shaking fists. There had to be something I could do to warn Archer and Danny—something I could do to protect them. Mother clearly hadn't tried to stop that woman from tossing me in here, as painful as it was to admit it, so if my brothers were at risk, it wouldn't be *her* saving them from this place either.

I had to get out. It was my only option. Inescapable or not, this prison wouldn't be my grave. Archer's face appeared clearly in my mind, and I could almost feel Danny tugging at my hair. We'd assumed they were both free of magic, but that assumption no longer brought me any comfort. Until it was certain they weren't mages, they were in danger.

And I was here.

I blinked at the mist swirling around me, so cool against my hot skin that it stung. Outside the door, there hadn't been any mist. This place was different from the outside world, following its own set of rules. The dense mist caught the faint sunlight filtering through the trees, which reflected off it like blue-tinted glitter falling through the air.

The door I'd entered had already vanished, leaving nothing but deep forest, thick with vines and that stinging, blue mist. My heartbeat drowned out the crickets and the birds. Somehow, I'd not thought creatures as simple as crickets would live inside this magical fortress. The blue mist ebbed and whorled around the trees, moving as though independent of the wind.

A shiver raked my spine as a wave of mist blasted around me. I exhaled slowly, trying to keep my panic from rising again and taking over. I shook out my arms and spun in a circle, relieved that my muscles were once again obeying my own desires. Trees surrounded me. Hemlocks and oaks and pines and small saplings and dead, hollow logs but nothing unusual. Vines streaked from the ground to the branches above. The forest felt *too* normal—too mundane—to be an inescapable prison built by powerful magic.

I didn't detect a single threat. In a prison built to drive men insane, I'd expected monsters or imposing walls. But a quiet, dark forest? That was somehow more sinister. The anticipation mounted in my gut, twisting into my muscles and gnarling my composure until I was bent double, breathing fast.

"Get it together," I told myself. This place was designed to incite madness, but I wouldn't let it. I straightened up and lifted my arms at my sides. "You're not that bad."

What if that door in the forest had been a trick and I wasn't even in the real Labyrinth? What if that mage had sent me out here to scare me? Was I panicking for no reason?

I planted my fists on my hips, embarrassed at the possibility. If this was only the Imperial Forest and the door had been a hoax to scare me, it had worked. Royal patrols were nothing compared to whatever monsters truly lurked within the Labyrinth.

I felt foolish.

Except...the door I'd entered *had* disappeared. And this blue-tinted mist was new. So either she had an architect with her to manipulate this section of forest, or I really was in the maze. I liked the first option best.

Then I heard a sound like an animal crashing through the leaves. My blood turned to ice.

If even a third of the legends were true, whatever animal now approached me wasn't one I wanted to meet. Crickets might dwell here, but I wouldn't trust them not to carve tunnels through me if given the chance.

A thick vine encircling a tree caught my eye. I raced to it, grabbed hold, and began to climb. The tiny purple-red hairs on the vine suggested this was not one I should touch, but the animal sounds grew louder—snuffling and snorting accompanying crashing footfalls—as if the animal was stampeding over whatever lay in its path.

When I was too far from the ground to jump, the vine changed. It sprouted offshoots and curled into the empty air. I now clutched the vine in dazed terror, but the vine ripped free of the tree and lifted me. It continued branching and growing into an impressive web that stretched between three of the nearest trees and held me suspended over the forest floor.

I was too scared to move. My hands gripped the vine, afraid it might decide to twist me upside down and dump me off at any moment. The animal crashed through the space below me, and I yelped in shock.

A hog the size of a small pony charged the very place I'd been standing a few breaths ago. The tusks on its snout were the size of antlers, so large they nearly dragged on the ground. They sliced like scythes through the thick vines, severing them as easily as cooked noodles.

The animal stamped the ground beneath me, tossing its head and those massive tusks. With each wave of its head, the sharp points cut away the vines holding me up.

I felt the web of vines tremble and tilt.

The hog was going to cut me down from this strange hiding place and tear me to pieces.

Pulse thundering, I climbed. Each time I reached out for a vine, it grew a new shoot and lifted me higher. The hog continued to thrash. The vine continued to branch.

Each snort from below drew a whimper of fear from my throat. Each new vine that sprouted into my hands brought the faintest whiff of safety. Clutching the vine with all my might, I hoped the hog would see that I was too far to reach and would give up.

It might have only been a minute, but after what felt like an eternity, the hog finally admitted its defeat and, grunting, crashed away through the forest, leaving a broken tunnel of vines where it had departed.

My pulse raced, and my hands trembled.

Tears of relief trickled down my cheeks. I rested against the vines holding my body aloft, limp with the sudden removal of panic. The vines gave way, instantly shrinking back to their original form, and I plummeted to the ground.

I hit the forest floor with a *whump* that knocked the air from my lungs a second time. This time, however, I couldn't get up quickly. I rolled to my side and slapped the ground, unsure if my lungs would ever inflate again.

My eyes bulged as my head throbbed and my vision darkened at the edges.

As I writhed on the ground, desperate for breath, Archer appeared before me.

He walked with purposeful steps, glancing at the ground as he stepped over roots and brush. His long blond hair was pulled half back behind his head. He looked older, with facial hair and clothes I'd never seen. Leather straps crossed his chest, and he'd grown more muscular.

This was my brother in the future. Time must work differently here. And now, he'd also been thrown into the Labyrinth as I'd feared.

I pushed myself up onto my hands and knees, blinking away the fuzziness in my vision. As I blinked, Archer's appearance shifted, blurring into something unrecognizable. My chest burned from the lack of air, my crushed lungs unable to draw in a full breath.

"Archer?" I croaked.

The man stopped and fixed his eyes on me. It wasn't Archer. His face was wider, fuller, and dark with rage.

Fear gripped me, and I finally gasped and gasped again, drinking in the sweet air.

The mist licked my ankles and slithered over my arms, like it was alive. The blue mist had gained a silvery hue, which washed over my face, stinging my eyes. I blinked and was suddenly looking at myself, as if in a mirror. The image vanished when I blinked again, and I was once more staring at the approaching stranger.

But in that one flickering glance, I'd seen myself from where he stood. In that heartbeat, I'd sensed panic and sadness, but not my own—more like a pinching loss for someone I'd never met. A strange thought now fled my mind, a sliver of a memory, no more than a single impression: the vision of a woman's face, pale as if lifeless. Silver-blue mist pulsed away from me, then swirled around the man in violent little whorls.

I labored to my feet, but I didn't take my eyes off the stranger.

He lifted a bow from his shoulder and before I had time to duck, an arrow whooshed right by where my shoulder would have been if my lace dress hadn't snagged on a broken sapling and held me down.

I yanked my dress free with a shout and stumbled backward, my stupid dress hooking everything on the forest floor. The man nocked another arrow and aimed, but no vines lifted me to safety this time. Silvery mist encircled me, eager to smother me.

My terror morphed into anger and I screamed. I wasn't ready to die.

The man paused and peeked around the bow. "Who are you?"

I was heaving breaths too fast to answer. Despite his weapon aimed at my head, I couldn't help but notice his strong build and ruggedly handsome face.

"Did the king send you? What does he want now?" His voice was deeper than Archer's. It sounded raspy, as if rarely used.

"King?" I wheezed, stepping behind a tree. I couldn't outrun a grown man on my best day, let alone in this dress and these slippers. "He put me in here. If that's what you mean?"

When the man didn't respond, I peeked around the tree and yelped. An arrow *thunked* into the bark beside my face.

"That was a warning," the man called out. "Stay away from me."

"You're not going to kill me?" I asked from behind the tree.

After a pause, "Not if you stop attacking me."

My eyebrows pinched and I shook my head. "Attacking? I have no weapon. I doubt I'd be able to take you down with a silk slipper."

The man cleared his throat, and I dared another glance around the tree.

"I was referring to your magic," he said, his bow no longer aimed at my head.

I opened my mouth to tell him I didn't have any worthwhile magic, but I snapped my lips shut before admitting this to him. Maybe it was beneficial if he had a reason to fear me.

"I won't hurt you," I said, trying to lift my voice to a more confident volume.

He replaced the arrow in the quiver at his back, never taking his eyes off of me. "Then why is your magic smothering me right now?"

I nearly fell over as I leaned too far around the tree. "What are you talking about?"

He tilted his head and stared at me. The mist circled him like a tornado, obscuring his features in a bright whirlwind.

"I'm not doing that," I said, staring at the vortex around him.

A frown formed behind his scruffy beard. "Is that right?" His tone told me he thought I was lying. "I can tell that you are new here, so I'll give you just this once. Attack me again, and I'll treat you like I treat any of the other threats in this place."

My muscles tensed and I jumped behind the tree once again. "I promise I won't!" I shouted, hoping he would finally leave me alone. I couldn't attack him with magic if I tried, but he didn't need to know that.

I chanced another glance around the tree. He was walking away so silently that he made no noise at all.

A small tremor shook the ground beneath my feet, and I clutched the tree to stop from falling over.

"Oh, no you don't!" shouted the man as he leaned into a sprint.

At that very moment, a wall burst out of the dirt. The man leaped to clear it, but the rising structure clipped his feet, flipping him into what was likely a nasty spin.

The wall settled into place and I stood there, gaping at the now quiet stone structure. Unless he had catlike landing ability, he was probably in a lot of pain right now.

He'd aimed an arrow at my head. Maybe if he was incapacitated, that meant I was safer. But he had spared me, which meant I didn't want him to be dead. As I crept toward the wall, I couldn't stop envisioning him lying on the other side of the wall, paralyzed. The stones were covered in moss and vines as if the wall had been standing right here for decades.

My hands started to itch. Absently, I rubbed them on my dress.

A few steps away, a door materialized in the stone wall. If the man was hurt, maybe I should help him to prove I wasn't a threat to him. I tried the handle. The door pushed open easily, though a loud creak filled the misty forest all around. I froze at the sound, half expecting a monster to crash through the brush nearby.

Nothing moved.

I stepped through the door, leaving it open behind me, and searched the ground for the bearded man.

He lay in a heap by the bottom of the wall. My hands shot to my mouth as I stifled a gasp. He didn't move when I prodded him with my foot. Or when I shook his shoulder.

One arm was pinned beneath his broad chest, the other stretched out beside him. His mouth was squished open against the dirt, but he was somehow still attractive, if not more so now that he wasn't scowling at me. His bow had fallen off his shoulder, and the quiver had slung all its arrows and was now on the ground near his head, the strap tight under his neck. His face was turning purple. I slipped my fingers under the strap at his chin and pulled it over his head. His skin quickly returned to a normal tone. My fingers itched from where they'd grazed his beard.

There, now I'd helped him.

His massive shoulders rose and fell in tiny, shallow breaths, but otherwise, he didn't move.

He had a knife hilt poking out under his waist, but when I reached for his hips, I couldn't even budge him enough to grab the knife.

I shook out my hands, glancing around to see if anyone had seen me grab the man's waist.

The bow would have to do. I gathered the arrows and collected the weapon from where it had fallen in the leaves a few paces away.

Now armed, I gave him one final glance before turning back to the door. I didn't know anything about the others in this maze, but perhaps I'd meet someone who didn't want to shoot me. Perhaps then I could ask them about any possible ways to escape.

I felt bad walking away from the blond man, but I didn't know how else to help him, and I couldn't risk him waking up and deciding to stab me.

The door in the wall had vanished.

This place truly had no rules.

Without any better ideas, I walked along the wall, at least keeping one side protected from attacks. The vines, now as dormant as normal vines should be, hugged the trees with their little tendrils as if nothing had ever happened. But there was still a tunnel carved through the underbrush where the hog had disappeared.

My chest ached, my hands itched, and my heart throbbed with fear and the acute ache of missing my family. Thoughts of my brothers turned my mind to Silver Creek. If I could find the creek, perhaps I could find a way out.

It was a fool's dream. This was a maze, after all, built to contain the strongest of mages, intended to crack their magic and their minds. But I couldn't accept that I was never going home, never going to see my brothers again, never going to get the chance to protect them from this awful place. So I let my hope consume me. I would find Silver Creek, and I would get out.

5

As I hurried away from the fallen man, memories of the giant tusked hog plagued my mind, and I gripped the smooth wood of the bow with a sweaty palm. Both hands itched constantly now, as did my cheek where it had touched the fuzzy vine.

Whatever monster came at me next, at least I had a weapon now. I was no longer dead in the water.

Nagging thoughts buzzed like flies against the sense of comfort I felt holding a weapon. *Who was that man? How often do walls shoot out of the ground? Will he be all right—and if so, will he hunt me down?*

Questions were less concrete than the sharp arrows in the quiver.

I drew an arrow, then thumbed the fletching with nervous fingers. The long weapon felt foreign and clumsy in my untrained hands, tipping forward and backward as I attempted to nock a single arrow. The pointed end wobbled as my shaking hands fumbled the string into the notch. Finally, I was armed—armed but hardly dangerous.

I lifted the bow and aimed at a tree. All around, straight trunks reached into the heavens, so tall I couldn't see their tops. The bow was too large or my arms were too weak...or both. I heaved back on the arrow, lost my grip, and watched as the arrow flopped useless onto the ground a few paces away.

With a grunt, I snatched up the arrow and tried again. This time, I managed to pull the string taut, but I couldn't figure out exactly how to hold the bow. I'd never used one before. My straight arm buckled sideways, and the arrow shot off a stone's throw to my right.

"Oops."

I snapped my mouth shut and glanced around. A few moments later, I'd recovered the arrow and nocked it again. My arms ached and my hands itched, making my attempts to hold the bow even less graceful.

I didn't know what lurked in the woods, and shooting an arrow into the mist might cause more trouble. Lowering the bow, I kept the arrow nocked and ready. I'd practice more, but not now. Now, I needed to find water—and a place, perhaps up in a tree, where I might feel safer.

Thick, writhing mist blanketed the forest floor. High in the trees, wind hissed through the branches. Faint whispers too quiet to discern drifted through the fog and the trees and left my skin prickled with gooseflesh. As I walked slowly forward, clutching the bow, my heart tapped like drums, and my neck dripped with sweat. The air was cooler here, shadowed from the summer sun, but it was also thicker, full of moisture that clung to my skin and smelled of damp earth.

Beetles the size of housecats skittered across the leaf-strewn ground up ahead. Two. Three. Four. I froze. They either didn't notice me or they were already hunting something else. My gaze traveled, and I saw a figure—a woman, by the shape of her clothes and body—fleeing the massive beetles.

Icy dread cut through me. She was the second person I'd seen, and I'd only been here a short time. I'd rather not run into *any* of the criminals haunting this maze. Though admittedly, some of them would be innocents like me, thrown in here for their affinity for mind magic. The only problem was, I had no way of knowing who was a criminal and who wasn't.

Though shooting arrows at my head was perhaps a good enough indication.

But he spared me. The thought brought little comfort, given the threat he'd hurled at me.

I adjusted my course to the left. As I glanced back toward the beetles, I saw that the trees had moved. One twisted oak was standing closer. A split-trunk tree that had been at least twenty paces back the way I'd come now loomed directly over me.

My balance faltered and I teetered, overcome with nausea at the idea that everything I'd once held as truth might not apply to this place. Terrified that the trees might come to life and grab me, I aimed the arrow, but my trembling grip flitted between the trunks of the trees, pivoting back and forth too quickly to hit either of them.

Before I was ready, I let the arrow fly. It *thwacked* against the split-trunk tree and dropped to the ground. My brows danced expectantly upward as I waited for the tree to move again. It did not. As I tiptoed to collect the weapon, keeping two eyes on the tree, a hand shot out from the tree, pale, blueish, and translucent, and snatched the arrow, drawing it back into the tree's trunk. The only evidence of the movement was the swirling mist.

With a shout, I hopped backward.

So the trees *could* grab me.

I tossed out my plan of climbing a tree for safety and picked my way through the woods, careful to remain as far from the large trunks as possible.

The air chilled unseasonably for late summer as clouds thickened overhead. Alternately raking my nails over my cheek and my palms, I scurried through the trees like a fox fleeing a hunting party, desperately searching for dark green clusters of honeyleaf, an herb with healing properties. With the dimming light, it was difficult to spot the little green leaves that blended in so well.

Almost as distracting as the itch in my palms was the weight of the man's quiver slapping against my back, a constant reminder that I was literally running for my life in a maze designed to tear apart my sanity.

My palms felt like they'd had hot wax poured on them. The skin was pink and swollen everywhere the vine had touched me. It was too early for evening, but if trees could walk and sprout arms, I guessed night could fall whenever it wished in this place.

"Honeyleaf, honeyleaf," I chanted as I walked bent over, fingers spread out as I studied the undergrowth.

Trees danced in my peripheral vision, making it impossible to know if I'd been walking in circles or moving forward. I soon grew dizzy from the changing landscape...and walking hunched over. I dropped to my knees. Water. I needed water. My desperate search for the herb to cure my itch had left me blind to water sources I might have passed. Right now, I'd take a wet leaf to allay my thirst.

After rubbing my palms along the lace of my ruined dress a half-dozen times, I stood to continue my search. I never *saw* the trees move, but every time I turned my head to glance around, the trees were in different places than I remembered seeing them. This was the worst kind of maze; it had no rules.

Madness was easier to fall into than I'd realized.

I fisted my hands—which only hurt the tender skin—and willed myself not to cry. This place had been built with the magic of the Guilds, which meant it contained the power of every kind of mage...including the architects' power to move any item anywhere. I ground my teeth and exhaled, glaring at the trees. Once there was an explanation for the moving flora, it felt less impossible, less wrong.

I kept my fears at bay by focusing on the things that felt real: the crunch of dead leaves beneath my feet, the feel of the cool mist on my skin, the smell of earth and the faint stench of the leather strap around my shoulder. Several steps later, a branch snapped, and I whipped my head sideways, only to walk directly into a tree that hadn't been there a moment ago.

"How'd you get here?" I scowled at the tree.

"They ain't your friends." The voice came from close by.

Panicked, I searched the semidarkness with wide eyes.

A woman stalked toward me, from the mist between trees, her long red hair in a ragged pile on top of her head. She wore a plain dress with what had once been an apron tied around it. The apron was now torn above the knees and so dirty with stains—some of which looked eerily like blood—that it was a wonder she kept it on. Her face was young but pinched with worry, anger, fear—or all three. She carried a sharpened stick in one hand and walked with the deftness of a hunter.

I stumbled as I backed away, trying to grab an arrow.

"I won't hurt you," she snapped. "I'm not a monster. Not yet."

"Who are you?"

She stepped around me in an arc that left a wide berth between us. Perhaps she feared me as much as I feared her. "Just another trapped soul," she said.

I blinked and kept my mouth shut. I hadn't expected to see other people here. At least, not so many so quickly. Maybe there were more mind mages than I'd assumed, people thrown in here like me without a public trial—because I hadn't heard of *that* many criminal trials ending in a Labyrinth sentence.

The woman straightened up, planting the back of her hand on her hip. With her sharpened stick, she gestured at the trees.

"You don't know about the trees yet, so I assume you're new. But you've already found a weapon—the Labyrinth must like you."

Apparently, my mouth was on strike, but my bewildered expression answered for me.

"I recognize that bow," she added, squinting at the weapon.

"I stole it," I blurted.

Her eyes went wide. "Yes, you are certainly new. Your dress isn't nearly ruined enough." She let out a small chuckle. "Is that a wedding dress? A *fire mage* wedding dress?"

"Yes—no." I shook my head. "It's a wedding dress, but I'm not a fire mage, and I didn't get married."

Her pale brows lifted. "Of course you're not."

I wasn't sure what to make of that declaration, but I didn't have time to respond.

"Now, if you want to live through the night," she continued, "you'd best stay away from the trees. Don't bother climbing them unless they reach down and pick you up. They help as often as they hurt, and you never know which it's going to be. Best to let them alone unless you can control them."

"Control them?"

The woman shook her head in an annoyed way, as if she didn't have time for my questions. "They've been enchanted like everything else here."

That didn't offer any clarity whatsoever to her comment about controlling the trees. I assumed any tree that could grab an arrow was *enchanted*. But her comment about not trusting even the things that helped me did make sense. The vines had saved me, but they'd made my hands itch like crazy.

I glanced at the bow in my hand. Would it give me boils or would the payment for accepting this weapon be even worse?

"Does everything here have a price? If something helps, it also hurts?"

She made a funny, strained sound in her throat that sounded like a half-crazed laugh. "If something helps, honey, it's fairly likely it'll try to kill you next."

"Will you?" I asked, my voice a little shaky.

Her eyes went wide, then she stepped around me, her homemade spear at the ready. "No. If a person can tell you their name, they ain't gone yet."

"Gone?"

"Gone mad."

The woman slipped quietly through the brush, making no more noise than a bobcat, then as the mist began to conceal her form, she called over her shoulder. "I'm Edith Temple. Tell me your name, sweetheart."

I doubted I was even five years younger than her, but she spoke with the authority of one much wiser than I. "Vera Rivers."

"Terrible to meet you, Vera," she said with a half-smile.

I raised my brows.

"It's just what we say here. Everyone you meet is going to end up dead or mad, sooner or later." She walked onward. "Don't trust anyone unless they tell you their name," she called back, already vanishing in the mist. "And if you think you've found a way out, just remember, the Labyrinth always lies."

For a moment, I stared at the swirling mist, mind spinning with everything I'd already learned about the Labyrinth. When my mind snapped out of my temporary daze, I called out to her, but there was no response. The silent mist swirled and hugged my body, which only served to highlight how alone I felt in this forsaken forest.

My hands itched so badly that I was brought quickly back to the present. The sensation was so acute, so agonizing, I wanted to tear off the blistering flesh. Bleeding would be preferable to this burning itch.

Something as silly as an itch that wouldn't go away was one of life's most frustrating things. This place really did want to drive me mad.

"I won't break that easy," I said aloud.

On the breeze, I was almost certain I heard the words, *But you will*.

I awoke face down in the leaves. My hands were so enflamed and tender I could barely push myself off the ground. My mouth felt heavy on one side. My puffy cheek was so swollen that I could see it when I looked down. My throat burned, and my tongue clacked in my dry mouth. Despite the agonizing itch, thirst screamed louder than all other sensations.

I didn't remember falling asleep. The last thing I remembered was kneeling in the semidarkness, still hunting for honeyleaf. As I stumbled to my feet rather clumsily, I spotted a dark green clump of the herb I'd been hunting only a few steps away. I'd been so close!

I kicked the plant lightly with my toe. My mother's slippers were ragged and brown. They wouldn't last long. The leaves didn't explode with spiders or transform into a pack of wasps. They merely flopped sideways.

Tentatively, I bent down to examine it, trying to ignore my screaming thirst and my throbbing, shaking hands. I smelled the faint, sweet whiff of honeyleaf.

I tore off a handful of small pointed leaves. Relieved tears welled in my eyes as I used my elbows to crush the leaves against a nearby rock and gently smeared the pulp into my aching palms. Then, with careful fingers, I rubbed a little onto my cheek.

My sigh of relief was loud enough to startle a nearby bird.

Every muscle tensed, but for the moment, nothing else moved.

As the torturous itch soothed away, I set my gaze forward and determined not to stop until I found Silver Creek. The sun was high in the sky again, which meant I'd slept all night and part of the next day—if time obeyed any rules here.

The oak and beech trees didn't move as long as I watched them, but before long, it seemed as if I had walked into an orchard—a gnarled and ominous orchard full of dead dogwoods. Hundreds of these lifeless trees pointed their limbs toward an indifferent sky. Movement caught my eye, and heat flashed through my arms and legs. Tall, lanky shadows with hollowed cheeks and the signature red hats of the king's soldiers waltzed among the trees, slipping in and out of view and taking my breaths with them as they went. They didn't seem to be in any hurry, but were all moving toward me, slithering in and out of view so that it was impossible to count them. Their vacant yet venomous stares suggested they were hunting, and I was the prey. Several of them appeared more skeleton than human.

For a moment, I was too scared to move.

My throat stuck to itself, making it hard to breathe. I contemplated stuffing a fistful of damp dirt into my mouth just to suck out the moisture, but the creeping shadows drawing ever nearer were reason enough to turn and run. I skirted the outside of the maze of brittle dogwoods and skeletal shadows. Soon, I lost sight of them, and—thank the fates—it didn't appear that they were rushing to follow me.

My body needed water desperately, but at least the miserable itch was subsiding. I stopped to examine the blisters forming on the underside of my arms from where they rubbed against the boning in my lace dress. This was arguably the worst attire for a survival situation. My mother's slippers were slowing me down, but it was that or walk barefoot through nettles and the occasional knife-like broken hull of old walnut shells.

The faintest sound of trickling water met my ears. My entire body responded, and I lost a little of my composure as a happy gasp burst from my lips. Even my blood, as it pumped through my veins, chanted *water, water, water*.

The trickling grew louder. I was crying and laughing by the time I saw the creek, gurgling along in a spot of sunshine. It looked so happy and merry, I forgot entirely that I was in a place designed to drive me mad.

I dropped the bow and quiver and dove for the water, crashing to my knees and sucking the cold liquid into my open mouth. I choked, coughed, and drank more.

That's when the first flash of silver scales startled me.

My face was pressed down into the water before I realized something was holding me. I thrashed and grabbed, but my hands only slipped off the slimy, cold flesh. The creek was shallow, and my mouth filled with sandy water.

Bucking like a horse, I managed to pull my face out of the water in time for a single breath. I swallowed enough sediment in that one breath that I went down again choking and hacking. But I'd seen my attacker.

A silver-scaled woman less than half my size and trimmed with tiny fins wrestled me with strong hands. She had wet hair clumped with grasses and eyes like black orbs. Her grip slipped toward my neck, and I knew if she latched on, I'd be dead. I threw a punch where her small head should be but missed. Using my legs, I wrenched myself around until I was face up, preparing to land a solid punch to her jaw.

She splashed back into the water and sank partway down into the mud, like a salamander. Then she was at my throat again, shoving my head under.

I gulped in a mouthful of water. There was no way to clear my lungs. The ripples in the water reflected the sunny sky above, but I saw the outline of my killer. She was so small, yet I couldn't overpower her. I remembered with a jolt that I had a weapon on the shore. But I couldn't breathe, and both my hands were employed in trying to shove her off. She flashed pointed, dark teeth at me. I curled my spine and kicked my legs over my head, using a move that always worked to throw Archer off when he and I wrestled. Only this time, my heel connected with my attacker's temple.

She sailed off me, and I rose from the water, sputtering and seeing stars.

My ragged throat burned like hot irons had been shoved into it. Readying for the next attack, I scrambled away, spinning around in the shallow water. But the creature was gone. A small, circular ripple in the sand indicated something had vanished straight into the creek bed.

Then the ripples dissipated as clear water rushed along its merry way.

Wearing only one shoe now, I stomped out of the creek for the weapon lying uselessly on the shore. I slung the quiver back over my shoulder and snatched up the bow, first slapping myself in the face with the string and finally holding it upright. I tried to grab an arrow from the quiver, but the strap was too long, and the arrows hung nearly horizontal across my back. After swatting the air several times, groping for an arrow, a deep, reverberating laugh startled me so severely that I grunted and swung the tip of the bow out like a sword.

Across the stream, the blond man stepped into view.

"I'll gore you with this if I must. I'm not half bad with a blade."

He stopped chuckling, then tipped his head back and laughed. It was the kind of laugh that loosened the tension inside me and I instantly desired to join in. A chuckle bubbled up. I likely looked anything but dangerous in my sopping wet wedding gown and one slipper, but I quickly tamped down the near-laugh, smothering it with the fear that still clutched at my lungs.

His gaze leveled out, and he stared at me with dark eyes—dangerous eyes, like those of a hunter who'd spotted his prey. This was the Labyrinth, and I could trust no one. He was no ally, no matter that he'd spared my life. My breaths quickened.

"Then it's a shame you don't have a blade," he said, resting one hand on the hilt of the dagger at his waist.

He was gloating. Or threatening.

"Who are you?" I hissed.

"A trapped soul. Like yourself."

"That's what Edith said."

"It's what we all say." He nodded at the silt-clouded water. "Kelpies are nasty creatures."

"That was a kelpie? I never thought they looked like that."

He grunted. "It's always how I imagined them." He stepped down the bank, one hand resting casually on his knife. "I told you to stop attacking me." He drew the blade and twirled it with deft fingers.

"I'm not attack—"

A horrible image flashed through my mind. A battlefield. Bodies, so many bodies, lying motionless in the grass at my feet. They wore the dark green and gold uniforms of Bevon's royal army. Blood ran down from a long cut on my right forearm, dripping off my fingertips. In my hands, I held twin swords coated in red.

But they weren't *my* hands.

Then my shoulders shivered, and I was again staring at the trickling creek and one waterlogged slipper on the bank beside me.

The stranger charged toward me, splashing through the creek in three long steps. I braced myself and jabbed with the bow, but he swatted it away. In a breath, his knife was at my throat, and I was lying back against the dead leaves and broken twigs along the weed-choked bank.

"It seems you are lying," he spat.

6

His knee pinned my shoulder down, and I crammed my eyes shut so that I wouldn't have to watch his face as he killed me.

"I can't even do magic!" I shouted through clenched teeth in a last-ditch effort to save my own life.

He chuckled, the knife pressing harder, and a tear leaked out of each of my eyes. My brothers' faces floated through my vision.

Then the knife withdrew, and the pressure vanished from my shoulder. I pried one eye open. His knife was back in its sheath, and he held both his hands in his hair, staring at me in wide alarm.

I labored to my feet in my heavy, wet dress. "What was that? Are you trying to kill me or not?"

His voice whispered on the breeze, barely louder than the trickle of the creek. "I don't know. You tell me. Are you not deliberately breaking my spells?"

At his words, every hair on my arms stood up. He held my gaze, his pupils softening from pinpricks to a normal, less frightening size.

More to prevent myself from launching into breathless tremors than from any desire to continue a conversation with this maybe-murderous stranger, I took a deep breath and forced myself to say, "I can't do magic on demand."

His head tilted to the side, his chin jutting up in that appraising way attractive men surveyed a crowd. But unlike all the other attractive men I'd seen pass judgment on me, his gaze lingered. He didn't know what I was—a quarter mage with no real abilities, but I'd just told him I couldn't do magic on command. I didn't like the feel of his gaze, like he now knew everything he needed to know about me and found me wanting.

Then, with a jolt, I recalled Edith's words. "What is your name?" If this man was already insane, then reasoning with him would do no good. Perhaps that was why he assumed I was attacking him.

A small huff escaped him. It might have been a laugh, but it wasn't a happy one like earlier. "You may call me Ash."

I sucked in a loud breath. "That's almost like Arch—" I stopped myself, a little too late.

He looked nothing like Archer really, but his long blond hair and similar name pricked a chord in my heart. I turned away, pressing back a wave of unwanted emotion. A small ripple coursed through the mist hovering over the creek, as if I'd somehow repelled it with my burst of emotion. If this was Silver

Creek, then maybe Danny's fears of monsters in the water were not as ill-founded as I'd once thought.

"Vera Rivers," I said, my voice still ragged from the thirst and the almost-drowning.

"Hello, Vera."

His voice drew my eyes back to him once more. That greeting—hearing someone speak my name in this forsaken place—warmed my cold skin and sent a wave of calm through my tense muscles. Ash stared at me with an intensity that anchored me to the ground, and I didn't think I could move if I wanted to.

"You stole my bow."

I glanced at the weapon on the ground beside me. "I tried to take the knife, but you're heavy."

The corner of his mouth twitched. "I'll trade you, then." He started to unfasten the belt holding one of his knives. He had another strapped across his back and a small one sticking out of his boot.

"Why?" I stepped back, afraid he'd loop the leather around my neck instead.

Midway through untying the leather, he glanced up at me. His jaw worked as he studied me, but he said nothing. After another tug on the leather, the belt fell loose and he held it out to me.

Still waiting for an explanation, I took it.

Ash dropped his arms and pushed his damp sleeves up to his elbows. "I've been here a long time, and I've...made my peace with this place. At least, I thought I had. Until you showed up."

A breeze brought a chill to my wet skin. "What's that supposed to mean?"

Ash lifted the strap holding his canteen over his head and took a swig. Buzzing with thirst, I watched his Adam's apple bob as he drank.

"It means you're disrupting the magic here," he replied, extending the canteen to me.

I stared at it, the sticky burn in my throat overpowering my rationality that warned I shouldn't trust someone who'd held a knife to my neck. I snatched the canteen and drained its contents. Wiping the water from my chin, I handed him his empty container.

"Disrupting the magic?" I repeated. "I'm a quarter mage. I don't disrupt anything." So much for keeping this piece of information to myself. He needed to know I wasn't the one breaking spells.

He stared at me for so long I couldn't stop the heat from flaring up my neck and into my face. "The Labyrinth disagrees." He slung the canteen back over his shoulder.

Water ran in rivulets down the backs of my legs and dripped rhythmically from the ends of my hair as I contemplated his words. "You speak like the Labyrinth *thinks*." Maybe madness had already taken this man.

Eventually, he nodded. "It does."

Okay, I was talking to a madman. Only he didn't sound mad.

"This place has a mind of its own. The monsters sense your fears as easily as you do. And they always come." He'd moved a fraction of a step closer as he spoke, and I felt his breath as he added, "The monsters are not always nightmarish in appearance. They can be as subtle as a dream or a whispered word in your ear."

From this close, I could examine his bearded chin, his expertly shaped nose, his eyes that, when watching me like this, weighed heavy as anvils. The damp fabric of his shirt clung to his strong arms. He seemed more sinister and more handsome each time I looked at him.

"You're wearing the color of fire wives," he said. "But you claim you're not a mage."

I frowned. "I'm not a fire mage, and I didn't get married."

A twig under his feet snapped, and I jumped at the sound.

"My maternal grandparents were mages," I explained. "Nan was a mind mage, and Pop was a fire mage. I've never been able to do any mind magic, but I have occasionally done fire magic—never on demand and never consistently enough to be admitted into the academy."

The words spilled out, my razor-edged confession. It was both freeing and infuriating to admit this to a total stranger.

His eyes narrowed briefly. "Academy?"

My mouth opened and closed. If he didn't know about the magical academy, then he was either from a faraway kingdom or...or he'd been here *much* longer than I'd thought. But if that were the case, he'd be an old man. I shook the thought away.

"I'm not a mind mage," I said. "They threw me in here because they assumed I was. And I have to get out, because I'm afraid they'll do the same thing to my brothers."

Fear caressed my spine. Danny and Archer had to be warned, had to be saved. I glanced at the creek again. There must be a way out, no matter that no one in eighty years had found it. Now, more than ever, I wanted to believe those childhood fantasies that spoke of creatures slipping from the maze at night.

Ash studied me again, this time with an intensity devoid of mocking or mischief. He seemed curious, which was somehow more unsettling. People tended to avoid looking at me, and if they did look, their glances were often accompanied by poorly delivered insults.

"What?" I finally burst, unable to stand the silence.

"Come with me." He reached for my arm, but I jerked away from him, noting a small, straight scar on his forearm. His right forearm. "You're not what you think, Vera Rivers. And I can't let your magic keep breaking things around here."

"Breaking?" The only thing I'd broken was a few twigs. "I haven't broken—" My words stopped as I recalled the strange memories I'd seen the two times Ash had appeared. He'd accused me of attacking him with magic. I must have seen into his memories, somehow.

Then it hit me. Like a solid wall bursting from the ground and toppling me. The hands I'd seen in that flash of battlefield memory were Ash's hands. He'd been *in* the war that took place eighty years ago.

"You said you've been here a long time," I began, trying to gain the courage to say what I'd just concluded. "Tell me your name again," I said, voice shaking. "Your full name."

His expression darkened and he leaned toward me. "Figured it out, have you?"

The name I'd learned in class, the name everyone in the entire kingdom of Bevon knew and feared, whispered through my memories as I stared at this man's deep brown eyes.

"You're him. You're Henry Asher. The mage who started the war."

7

My head began to shake, first in small motions, then in increasingly larger movements. "No. It can't be."

He sighed and collected the bow and quiver from the ground. "Not many of the prisoners here have discovered this information. I would prefer if you kept it to yourself."

He wasn't even denying it.

I backed away, wrapping the leather belt around my waist with shaky hands.

"Don't walk away," he said.

"Don't talk to me!"

He folded his arms. "I could make you come with me, but I'd rather not."

Gaping at him, I tried to fill my lungs, but my breaths had gone shallow once more. "You didn't have a problem controlling entire armies in the war."

His expression darkened. "And people can't change, can they?"

I paused, one hand holding tightly to the knife hilt at my waist. "You murdered thousands of people."

"It was war."

To that, I had nothing to say. My throat had closed up so that only ragged, wheezing breaths sawed through me.

"You may think what you wish about me, but I cannot let you go."

I pulled the knife out, knowing now that he could make me stab it into my own stomach if he wished. This was the villain that had caused mind magic to become illegal. How he was still alive, I didn't want to know.

"I'll attack you again!" I warned, my voice weak and uncertain. At the thought that I'd considered this man attractive, I heaved with disgust.

He chuckled. "That's exactly why I can't let you go. You see, your fitful magic is causing me problems, and as you apparently have no control over it, I will just have to teach you how to use it." He rubbed his hands over his beard. "For my own peace of mind."

"You don't deserve peace of mind!"

He recoiled in mock offense. "You do realize that if I go mad, every spell my mind sustains will also break."

A shudder raced across my cold skin. "You control the monsters?"

His lips turned down. "No. They are controlled by locked spells that no longer need my energy to sustain them. They feed on fear, and I can't stop them. But I can distract them, redirect them, and occasionally kill them with weapons. I can't, however, break through the locked spells around them." He stared at me for a long moment. "Your magic is breaking the spells I have in place here to keep people *safe*."

I threw my hands up. "Wait. You're telling me *you* keep people *safe* here? You made the monsters. You're the reason we're all here!"

To my surprise, his chin fell and he let out a long breath. "Anything else?"

I blinked at him.

"You must learn to control your magic, Miss Rivers. If you do not, then I can't help you or anyone else tossed in here. You are woefully untrained, and the longer you remain that way, the greater the danger for everyone in this prison."

He waited for me to speak, not moving any closer or reaching for any arrows.

Mist licked at my arms and cheeks. I shivered from the cold, despite the fact that it was summer outside the Labyrinth. In here, even the seasons didn't obey the rules.

"I won't let *you* teach me. You're..." I couldn't willingly follow this man. He'd fought the king for the throne all those years ago and gobbled up other people's magic all because he wanted power. He was wicked and vile.

But he hadn't killed me when he had the chance.

He lifted both his hands, palms toward me. "Listen, I understand you don't trust me. At least let me take you to someone else who can teach you how to control your magic. Will you do that or will you keep gawking at me?"

I opened my mouth, shut it, then opened it again. "I'm a quarter mage. I can't learn how to control my magic."

He chuckled, but it sounded more annoyed than amused. "You're wrong. Magic like that is not from a quarter mage, no matter what you might think. Now, please, let's go. Your magic is starting to get out of hand again."

His words hit me like I'd been slapped. *Magic like that.* All around, the mist swarmed in increasingly agitated spirals, as if sensing the rising tension.

"How do I know you won't kill me on the way?" I asked. "Edith told me the Labyrinth always lies. If you're the keeper of this place, perhaps you're lying too."

He knelt and placed one hand on the ground, as if petting a dog. "Sage advice, but I'm the one who told *her* that. It's to Edith that I plan to take you. She can teach you what you refuse to learn from me. The Labyrinth senses that your magic is tampering with it. And I've seen what the Labyrinth does to mages who attract its attention."

"You mean *your* attention."

He stood and stormed forward, his eyes flashing. "Think what you want about me. But a wall is about to shoot up on the other side of this creek, and we'll be forced to walk a day out of the way if we don't move right now."

As his words ended, I felt the ground tremble.

He tugged my arm forward, and I didn't think, I just ran, leaving both slippers behind.

We splashed through the creek, and I lost my footing on the other side. The ground was shaking in earnest now, and I couldn't get my balance. Ash scooped me up with one arm and hauled me up the small, steep bank. With a shove, he pushed me forward so hard that we fell and rolled on the ground right as a stone wall burst from the forest floor. My dress snagged on the rising stones, tearing a little.

I lay on the ground, breathing in ragged gulps, as dirt and leaves rained down over me.

Ash hopped up beside me, then extended his hand toward me. "We'll need to hurry. The Labyrinth doesn't like it when I help people, and it's trying to cut me off from you. We shouldn't wait around."

I stared at it, thinking of the memory of the blood on his hand, of the stories I'd heard in class of the atrocities his magic had committed.

"Like it or not, I'm your best bet right now," he added. "And besides, I know where all the monsters are at all times. And there's one headed this way."

I slapped my hand into his, and he pulled me up. For a second, I stood chest to chest with him. Then together, we turned and ran.

⚬

As we ran, my bare feet, softened from the water, stepped on what felt like every upturned walnut shell and broken twig.

I stopped to examine a small puncture wound from a jagged sapling half-buried with leaves when I heard laughter.

Not a sound I'd expected to hear in this place.

Ash turned and stared at my foot. "Ignore the laughter. It just means the Labyrinth is testing you."

I narrowed my eyes at him. "You mean *you're* testing me."

He huffed in annoyance. "Your history books told you all you need to know about me, is that right?"

"Yes."

He rolled his eyes. "I'm sure the king enjoyed commissioning those books. For now, we need to keep moving. Can you run?"

I set my injured foot down and winced.

"Climb on."

"What?" My mouth hung open as he turned his back toward me and lifted his arms. "Never in a million years."

"Think touching me will rub my wicked ways into your virtuous skin?"

I balked and marched past him, shoving my pain aside.

"Fine," he grumbled. "You can choose to believe what the king's version of history told you about me. It's this way," he added, storming off to the left.

As we picked our way through the trees, I pondered his words. The king had defeated Henry Asher eighty years ago, banishing him and his dark magic into this dreadful prison. The villain we'd learned about was ruthless and power hungry and vile. Not the type to spare lives or offer piggyback rides to ladies with sore feet. But if this place was designed to drive me mad, I wasn't about to trust its maker.

I darted my eyes back and forth so often, scanning for lurking monsters, that I was nearly getting dizzy. I pinched my lips and tried to snuff the fear that wafted off of me like candle smoke. It was no use. The creature from the water had terrified me, and nearly drowning had left its mark on my mental state. I wanted to find water without murderous monsters in it. And a place to hide. And a new outfit. And a way out. And an entire cake wouldn't hurt either.

One thing at a time.

We walked for what felt like an hour without anything attacking. My feet hurt so badly—each step was a hobble that almost ended in me falling to the ground. But I was too proud to admit this to Ash.

I concentrated on the feel of the ground beneath me, forcing my awareness away from the pain in my feet. If a monster chased after me right now, I'd be hopeless if I couldn't run.

Years ago, I'd cut my hand with a kitchen knife while peeling potatoes for Mother, and I'd learned that I could ignore pain by shoving it out of the forefront of my mind and locking it away. After several breaths, the pain diminished, and I sighed.

Ash eyed me with a raised brow and looked me up and down. "Already getting comfortable here?"

"No," I huffed.

The silvery mist appeared like rain, falling toward the earth in little rivulets that sank into the ground. Now that I'd gotten a handle on my pain, I could focus on our surroundings. Vines hung innocently from trees and birds fluttered away in fear. At a glance, this forest was no different from any other I'd seen—and that made the anticipation so much worse.

As I stepped over a fallen tree, my dress caught and a ripping sound accompanied my fall.

"Excellent."

Ash turned around so fast, blade drawn, that I flinched. His eyes flicked from me to the forest and back to me.

"Oh," he said, stepping toward me as he tucked the blade back into his boot.

Lifting my damp, leaf-encrusted skirts, my hand bumped something hard. I shifted and saw a small stone opening in the ground—a well.

I'd knocked off the flat rock that had covered the well, and my dress had snagged on the rough-cut edge of one of the stones. Sitting beside the well was a small cup attached to a long string. For a second, I stared dumbly. The well hadn't been there a moment before.

Ash chuckled. "Ah, the well." He turned in a circle, his hand slipping around the knife hilt once again.

I spun in the leaves and stared at the tiny structure. Something was etched into the edge of the well. Smearing some of the lichen and dirt off the stones, I scooted around until I found the beginning of the phrase. "To take a drink, you must pay the price," I read aloud.

"Yes, and I expect the payment will be due soon."

I clambered for the cup, tossed it into the well, and drew up cool, refreshing water. My body didn't care what the price might be. I would die without water anyway.

Without hesitation, I drank three cups full of the cool, slightly earthy-tasting water. I poured a fourth over my hands. And a fifth over my face.

"You aren't afraid of the price?" asked Ash, a curious hitch in his voice.

"I'm with you. The maker of the monsters. What could be worse than that?"

He inclined his head, but before he could respond, a crashing sound stopped my heart.

I leaped up, dropping the cup and groping for the dagger Ash had given me. It felt much better in my hands than the bow and arrows.

Long red hair flashed in the mist-brightened sunlight.

"Edith?"

She sailed over a fallen log and dove for the cup, but it had vanished...along with the well.

"Blast!" she roared, slapping the leafy forest floor with both hands. She knelt a moment, rocking back and forth, before looking up at me. "You pleased the Labyrinth. Good job."

Dazed, I said nothing in return.

She stood slowly, nodding at Ash. He nodded at her in return. "I've been on the run since late last night. Wolves this time. I hate the wolves here. They're..." Her face shook with a disgusted tremor.

My eyes raked the woods behind her.

"Oh, no, I lost them some time back. They tire of me, eventually. I'm not afraid of them, you see. I hate them, but only because they run me ragged." She bent double and heaved several breaths. "The water...I haven't seen a well since yesterday."

"How did you know I'd found one?"

"I've been following you since the wall. A few of us have been."

Again, my eyes flashed to the forest all around. I saw no one. A glance at Ash told me he wasn't surprised at all by her words.

Edith straightened and pushed her hair out of her face. "The Labyrinth always helps the newest ones the most." She snorted. "It draws you in, makes you think it's friendly. We track down the newcomers, and they almost always lead us to water. Or food. Or shelter. Or whatever the Labyrinth decides to give you to make you trust it." Her eyes flickered to the dagger in my hands. "I see Ash has helped you too."

I stared down at the place the well had been. Anger flared in my chest at the thought that this place was some kind of grand game with no winner. Pass a test, get a prize. But never try to leave.

"What do you eat here? I'm starving," I blurted, hopeful that Edith or Ash could share the secrets of survival in this place.

"Mm-hmm. I bet you are." Edith's grin was slightly crooked and dimpled on one side. "Good thing I followed you then, because I have food. And someone you might want to meet." She pursed her lips at Ash. "Why are you here?"

He tucked his knife back in its sheath. "She needs training. I assumed you could help."

"Training?" repeated Edith, eyeing me with curiosity.

"I've never been able to do magic at will," I admitted. "And he thinks I'm attacking him with my magic."

"She is," he growled.

A strange sensation flowed down my spine, and my head felt momentarily fuzzy. I blinked and stepped backward, throwing my arms out to balance my unstable legs. My hand knocked into Ash's chest, and I jerked it back toward me.

Ash stepped forward and shouted at Edith, "Don't!"

Instantly my head cleared.

"Sorry," Edith said to Ash, eyes wide. "I was just trying to get a read on her."

"Were you just in my head?" I clenched my fists at my sides as memories of another woman controlling my body flushed a heated panic through my veins.

Edith waved a hand like this idea was trivial and leaned forward. "For all I know, you're a new kind of monster meant to look like a newcomer." I scoffed, but she continued, "But the monsters don't let me in like that. I've yet to feel the consciousness of a monster here. It's almost like...almost like they aren't even real." Her voice faded a little, and her expression slackened, but only for a heartbeat. Then she jabbed her thumb at Ash. "It seems he doesn't want me to see what's in your head."

I lifted a brow at Ash, but he'd turned away. *She doesn't know.* I considered spilling his secret right then and there, but it would do me no favors. He could likely eliminate us with magic long before he needed his bow and arrows or his knife. And besides, I was so hungry I could eat a whole chicken, so I stepped toward Edith, stomach growling.

"You said you have food?"

"Ah, not here." She lifted a warning hand. "The others might be hungry too, and I don't have enough food for all of them."

My eyes flitted between the trees and my heart rate doubled.

"You won't see them. After a few weeks in this place, you learn to move without sound, to breathe without moving, to listen like a rabbit." She waved me forward. "Can you walk?"

I glanced at my feet, where dirt and a little bit of dried blood stuck to the skin between my toes. "I...I'm fine."

Her brows lifted, and Ash shook his head.

"I walked barefoot at home a lot." It was true, but it also sounded less strange than telling her I could shut off my ability to feel pain.

"Okay, then," she said, shaking her head slightly. "You've got a lot to learn, and the Labyrinth always punishes you after it provides."

"The well warned of a price to pay," I replied, pulse quickening in anticipation.

"That's right."

A shadow moved in the trees, and I sucked in a breath. Edith turned and waved me to follow, but Ash merely stared out over folded arms at the misty forest, a warden observing his charges.

"Why are you offering me food, but not them?" I asked as I hurried after Edith, careful to avoid rocks and roots on the ground.

She chuckled. "You haven't tried to kill me yet. They all have." She snapped fierce eyes back at me. "And besides that, I was sent to fetch you."

"By who?"

Edith lifted her pale brows. "You'll see."

I swallowed. I had no reason to trust her—or whoever sent her to *fetch me*—but my reason was frayed at the edges, and the empty ache in my stomach drove me to follow her through the swirling mist.

I had hoped Ash would stay behind now that I'd found Edith. But he slipped silently after us, catching up in a matter of steps.

"You said you would leave me with Edith," I reminded him, careful to keep my voice low.

"I'll leave you at the fort, not before." As he walked, he nocked an arrow, keeping the bow low beside him.

"Fort?"

He didn't answer.

This place was not the maze I'd expected. It was a mental game, its rules built by magic. Nothing was trustworthy, not even the kind woman leading me through the woods or the man following close behind me. They might help today, but tomorrow, I wouldn't trust them. I would eat, then I would get back to searching for a way out.

"How many others are there?" I asked as I picked my way through thorny vines.

Edith glanced over her shoulder at me. "Twelve, by my last count, but you make thirteen. Although, by now, I'm sure Benny and Rita have...well, I'm sure they couldn't tell you their names if you were to run into them." Her voice thickened with sadness.

"Have they gone mad?"

She nodded, her lips pressed in a thin line. "They're what we call the Nameless now. The Nameless are almost as great a threat to you as the monsters themselves."

"Are there a lot of Nameless here?"

Edith stopped and turned to fully face me. "Hundreds."

After Edith's comment, I couldn't take a step without glancing to my left and right. I looked up at the trees, back behind me, and then scanned the surrounding forest, breathing much faster than our pace required. Fear, palpable as it rose in my belly, threatened to turn me to stone. I fought to keep moving, to keep trusting Edith. I had no food and had never killed an animal in the forest with a blade before. I also didn't trust the edible flora in this place, so I had no other choice than to trust the woman in front of me. Ash I did not trust, but I liked the idea of his arrows hitting any approaching monsters.

Several times, Edith stopped to urge me along. "Come on. The monsters can smell your fear. Heck, *I* can almost smell it."

Ash huffed in agreement.

She patted the torn lace sleeve of my dress and pressed me onward. "Keep walking. It's not long now until we reach the fort."

As we walked, my mind flashed with images of the old fort in Westburg, an imposing structure with turrets and an armory, that once served to save the royal family from attackers. Though I doubted Edith's fort was as strong as the king's, I hoped it was truly safe. I longed for a moment free from the flutter of panic in my lungs.

Before long, the hunger pangs in my stomach sounded like veritable beasts. Edith increased her pace, forcing my bare feet to scamper faster over the forest floor. I had to tamp down thoughts of the pain in my feet that kept threatening to overtake me. Who knew there were so many broken things in a forest? So many sharp edges waiting to pierce human flesh?

"Faster," Ash urged, his own breaths quick and his eyes wide as he pushed me from behind. "They're coming."

I didn't stop to ask what was coming. Edith charged forward, leading the way.

I ran. Moving faster made my feet hurt less. I barely touched the fragmented acorns and small, half-hidden rocks. My eyes scanned the ground, careful to step where I wouldn't turn an ankle. The brush was thick, and the nettles gathered in ever-denser patches until we were entirely surrounded by thorns.

Ash slung the bow over his shoulder and started chopping at the brambles with a machete that had been stowed in a long leather sheath at his back. Edith whipped out a dagger from beneath her apron and began to hack at the thorns methodically, like she'd done this before. I drew Ash's blade and attempted to do the same, though it took me two chops to cut through one of the vines.

Ash hacked in an *X* motion, chopping a thin path through the nettles. They grew back just as fast.

After a few minutes, Edith huffed angrily. "It's no use!" She stuffed the dagger back into its hidden sheath. "These vines aren't responding to my magic—they've been locked against magical attacks! We have to climb over."

"Hurry!" shouted Ash as he backed up. "I'll hold them off." He took off back the way we'd come.

I tried to swallow, but my throat closed up. Without warning, Edith launched herself onto the bramble patch like a cat. She crashed down into it, thorns tearing her sleeves and drawing blood. She let out a small yelp but pressed on, thrashing her arms and grabbing the vines with her bare hands.

I bent down and pulled the outer layer of my lace dress up over my shoulders. Tucking the fabric tight against me, I charged into the brush. The thorns bit at my dress, but very few poked all the way through to my skin. The layered skirts protected my legs from some of the sharp points, although I could feel scratches tearing the skin on my arms. Edith shot me an amused look and nodded her approval.

Then the vine wrapped around my ankle, and I went down, hands splayed out to shield my face from the thorns.

"Edith!"

A large thorn pierced my palm until the red tip glistened above my knuckles. Several other thorns lodged in my stomach and thighs. I yowled. My head swam at the sight of the blood oozing from my hand. Using all my mental energy, I closed my eyes and shut my mind to the pain. Soon, my hand barely hurt, and I yanked it off the thorn, tucking it against my stomach as warm blood leaked out.

Edith thrashed through the nearby vines.

A low rumble in the distance indicated something very large was quickly heading our way. A shriek from Edith brought a wave of fear so palpable it eclipsed my remaining pain for one breath. I couldn't move.

Edith shouted, "As soon as you're free, run. Don't look back. Stay straight and you'll reach a big tree—wide as a house. There's a girl there. Name's Ferrier. You shout her name, and she'll let you in."

I tried to speak, but my voice was caught in my burning, aching throat.

Thundering hoofbeats approached. Had the creature trampled Ash?

In a heartbeat, the vines caging me withdrew, pulling free from my skin, and I flopped the rest of the way to the ground.

I scrambled to my feet, cradling my punctured hand against my stomach. I lurched forward, glancing back and forth for Edith.

"The enchantment broke! Run!" she screamed.

Blond hair caught my eye right before the snout of an enormous bull moose burst through the trees. Ash was running back toward us, behind the creature.

The moose charged directly toward me, and I bolted for the nearest tree, hopping behind it as the massive animal tore past, splintering the trunk with the edge of his antlers. My heart beat madly, and I breathed in ragged terror. The moose's eyes held a reddish tint, and its shiny, black antlers were wide as a river boat and tipped with knife-like points.

Turning away, I watched in horror as Edith tripped and hit the ground hard. She lifted her head up and then flopped back onto her stomach.

The moose charged.

I dove for Edith, and rolled, bringing her limp body with me. The vines sprang to life again, slithering across the forest floor toward us.

Her eyes popped open. "I said don't look back!"

She shoved me off and grabbed my hand. It was so slippery with blood that she lost her grip and stumbled. With wide eyes, she glanced at my blood-slicked fingers.

"Run!"

Her word was a shriek, and I didn't need to be told twice. The vines reached for my legs once more, and I heard the thunder-clap hoofbeats of the charging moose. I hopped sideways, behind a tree, as the animal shot past once more.

A warm hand grabbed my arm. "Get on!" Ash pressed his back to my chest.

I climbed on before I knew what I was doing, clinging for dear life. Then he tucked into a sprint, following Edith's flame-red hair. His machete sliced through the vines as they shot upward all around us.

"Coming in!" Edith shouted from a few paces ahead. "Two!"

Two ropes dropped from a high branch. Edith launched herself at one, quickly wrapping her ankle around the rope and shimmying up. I hopped off of Ash's back and he was up the rope in a matter of seconds.

I grabbed hold of the rope, but my pierced hand was of no use.

The moose splintered branches and logs as it stampeded toward me. I wrapped the rope around my shoulder and kicked my feet up at the trunk. With all my willpower, I walked up the trunk, aware that someone above was pulling the rope as well. The massive antlers passed under my back, tugging at my long hair.

I was nearly to the lowest branches when my strength gave out. My feet slipped and I tilted forward, my chest knocking into the trunk of the tree. I held my weight with one arm for a second, but my fingers were already losing their grip.

Then Ash's strong hands grabbed my forearm and hauled me upward.

8

I stared up at Ash. He hefted me into the tree, laying me gently on a wooden platform canopied with leaves.

I opened my mouth to thank him, but only a broken croak emerged. My blood had soaked into the collar of his shirt. He was the villain in all the stories. And yet he'd just saved my life.

He shook his head, turning to take something from Edith, who was perched behind him. A cup, brimming with water.

I took it with trembling, grateful hands and sucked it dry, dribbling a third of it into my lap. Ash reached for the empty cup, his gaze flickering to my wounded hand and the blood on my abdomen. His dark eyes flashed before he looked away.

"That was close," Edith said, taking the cup from Ash.

The moose was still snorting and pawing the ground below. Its antlers shook the massive tree. Tipping sideways, I yelped and reached for something to steady me, but there was only Ash. His arm shot out, grabbing my hand. For a brief moment, I held his stare as I straightened up once again. Then his fingers slid from mine, and he scooted back, allowing Edith to come forward.

I glanced at the platform beneath us, which was composed of young trees stripped of branches and strapped together. I inhaled sharply and took in my surroundings. I wouldn't have actually fallen. More logs, also bound together with twine, stretched around the trunk. The larger branches poked up through the platform, but there was enough space for several people to sit comfortably. A pale face trimmed with orange-red hair peeked at me from behind one of the upward-reaching branches.

Edith grabbed my hand and examined it, clicking her tongue. "That was *too* close. I told you to leave me behind!"

My attention snapped back to her. "I couldn't leave you there." Only now that I wasn't outrunning a bull moose did I notice the throbbing pain in my hand and feet had returned and the puncture wounds along the front of my body smarted. I winced as Edith turned my hand back and forth.

She blew out a long breath and stared at me with a pinched brow. "Thank you."

I glanced back at Ash, who lurked in the shadows of the leaves, and the shy, young face still watching me from across the platform.

"I'm just glad I found you," Edith wheezed, still breathless from the chase.

"Why's that?" I asked.

Edith whipped her head around to look at Ash, then met my gaze again, red hair whirling like flames around her ember-bright eyes. "Because she told me to."

"She?" My eyes flicked to the young girl crouching behind a branch.

Edith shook her head. "Not my sister. Revera."

I choked at the name. I only knew one person with that name, the name that inspired my own. Revera Oslow was my grandmother's name. Edith rose and stepped across the makeshift platform, where a curtain that might once have been a skirt draped down, forming a partition. Edith lifted the curtain. A person lay on a small arm of the platform that reached out between the thick branches.

"She's here."

My pulse fluttered, and I scooted forward, drawn to the prone form. I didn't feel comfortable enough to stand on the platform, so I crawled on my knees, careful to keep my bleeding palm lifted.

When I saw the face angled toward me in the mottled sunlight, I sucked in a breath that quickly turned to a quiet, joyful sob.

Nan looked up at me with her kind smile and reached for me. Tears leaked down her soft, wrinkled cheeks as I grasped her hand.

"I thought you...we all thought you were..." I couldn't say the word, not now that I knew it was untrue. Nan's funeral, the tears I'd cried...they suddenly felt like a violent blow.

"I know, my dear." Nan's voice was weak and fragmented, but it still brought a wave of joy to me that sent fresh tears down my face. "The king and his Guild puppets didn't want anyone knowing what he had done to me. They rightly believed it would anger you, and they didn't want you angry with him."

"Of course I would have been angry. I'm angry now!" I slammed a fist into my lap. "Why did he throw you in here? Wait, why would the king worry about *me* being angry?"

Nan's eyes closed and opened again, so slowly that my heart skipped a beat. She looked so tired and frail compared to the woman I'd known. If the king had thrown her in here back when we'd all thought she'd died, then Nan had been in this nightmarish place for two whole years.

She offered me one of her characteristic closed-lip smiles. "That will take some explaining, my dear."

"I'm not going anywhere."

Nan glanced at my hand, which was still bleeding, and the blood that had soaked into the lace bodice of my dress where I pinned my hand under my elbow.

"I believe Asher is preparing a healing salve for that."

My chest pinched a little at the name, and I wondered if Nan knew his true identity. But I didn't want to burden my grandmother with this knowledge, not knowing how she might react. She'd been trapped in here for two years—there was no telling the toll it had taken on her.

"His name reminds me of Archer," I said with a twang of sadness.

Nan nodded, her hair tangling against her makeshift pillow of folded garments. "He shortened it to Ash when I told him the same thing two years ago. He didn't want me to feel unnecessary sadness every time I used his name."

I blinked in stunned silence.

"But despite his good intentions, I kept calling him by his real name," Nan said with a smile. "It is just my way." She sighed.

I looked around for Ash, but he'd disappeared. Edith and the younger girl remained on the platform, mere steps away, but they'd turned away to give us a little privacy.

"But you asked about the king," Nan said, drawing my attention back to her. "There's much to explain, but I'm afraid it should wait until you are less exhausted."

"Nan, please. Why was the king *afraid* of me?" My heartbeat tapped like a soldier's drumsticks inside my chest.

She offered the hint of a smile. "You have a unique kind of magic, Vera. It's really my fault, I suppose." Here she paused, mouth ajar, an almost apologetic frown on her face. "My magic is also unique, and highly valuable. I'm what is called a lock. It means I can lock spells in place without having to feed them constantly with energy."

Ash had said he too could lock spells in place.

"Mind mages like me were recruited by the Guild before the war. I, of course, was too young at the time, and when I manifested my affinity after the war, mind magic was already banned. I never received proper training, but my father allowed me to practice on him. When Rebecca was born and never manifested any magic, I knew that the unique kind of magic I had would pass to one of my grandchildren."

"How could you know that?" I asked. "Magic isn't always passed on." My legs pressed uncomfortably against the wooden boards beneath me, but Nan's words kept me fixed to the spot.

"I suppose I didn't know for certain, but I never doubted that it would," she said. "The thing about a lock is that when their magic is passed on, it can change, and that person becomes what is known as a key. And I assume you can riddle out what a key can do?"

Adrenaline surged under my skin as the truth hit me. "Unlock spells."

Ash had accused me of breaking locked spells, but I didn't even know how to *do* magic. Much less purposefully unlock a spell.

Nan nodded, another close-lipped smile wrinkling her face.

My mind spun. A dark presence at my right shoulder startled me, and I flinched. Then Edith stepped up beside me, holding onto a branch over her head for balance.

"We need to bandage that hand."

I hadn't realized how badly I was trembling until I glanced down at my punctured hand. I nodded shakily.

"She'll be back in a moment, Revera. We'll bring you some broth in a little while."

I stepped back down to the wider part of the platform and nestled against the massive tree trunk, as far from the edge as possible. My lace dress had so many tears, it looked like I'd been in a fight with a large cat—and lost. My chest heaved up and down, but I couldn't seem to calm my breathing.

Edith squatted on her ankles, ripping off a long piece of cloth from the bottom of one of the curtain-like partitions. "Your Nan is a remarkable woman," she said. "Without her, I'd be dead."

Blinking in surprise, I glanced at Ash to see if he had anything to say about Nan, but he wasn't watching me. He was leaning against a sturdy branch with one arm propped up on an overhead limb and peering down at the forest floor, which had grown quiet. I was momentarily struck by how strong he looked. Admitting he was handsome felt wrong now that I knew who he was, but I couldn't forget the way I'd clung to him, trusting him to save my life—and he had. Movement to my right sent a nervous twitch through me, but it was only the young girl finally emerging, crawling on her hands and knees across the platform.

"She's the reason we're all still alive," the girl said, her voice high and a little scratchy. She might have been ten years old, entirely too young to be in this monstrous place.

Edith glanced over at her. "My sister, Ferrier."

The girl sat cross-legged an arm's length away, a bright smile on her freckled face. Then she dropped her gaze to her lap. "The Labyrinth had forced me away from Edith, but your Nan found me. She brought me back to my sister."

Edith patted Ferrier on the shoulder. "We owe Revera a debt we cannot repay. I told her I'd met a woman named Vera Rivers, and she told me to go after you. So I did."

I nodded, still somewhat in shock at finding Nan here, but a burst of wind rustled the tree limbs, and my eyes followed the branches as a wave of fear coursed through me.

Noting my worried look, Edith said, "The tree won't move. Your Nan's got it under control, and her magic never breaks."

"She's a lock," I whispered, trying to absorb it all. *And I'm a key.*

My magic might be unique, but it was fitful as a two-year-old. I bit my lip as Edith shifted so she could sit cross-legged beside my outstretched legs. I was itching to speak to Nan more, to learn about locks and keys, but my wounds were screaming for attention. I thought my pulse was finally going to have a chance to slow after escaping that moose, but it picked up tempo as if I were still on the run. Edith snapped her fingers at Ferrier, who handed her a small tin. My stomach growled loudly.

"Oh, food. That was the whole reason you followed me." Edith pressed a hand to her forehead. "We won't have long before something else comes for us. We need to doctor that hand, but we also need to cook."

Ash stepped across the platform. "I'll do that. You get the food."

Edith shot him a skeptical look, but then nodded gratefully and descended one of the ropes to the ground below.

Heart hovering in my throat, I tensed as Ash folded his legs and sat beside me, his knee brushing against my thigh. He took the bandage and the tin, and then he took my hand, setting it on his leg.

I tried not to move even when I breathed. Ash's warm, calloused hands lifted my wrist and my entire consciousness narrowed until the only reality was where his skin touched mine.

From the tin he scooped a mash that smelled of brightberry and whistletop blooms—magical plants created by the Guild for medicinal purposes. I never imagined they'd grow here. With one finger he gently tapped the ointment over my wound on both sides of my hand. His other hand held my wrist still.

I chewed my lips and hoped he couldn't feel the tension roiling off me like steam. I dared not look up at him, lest he see how much pain and nervousness I was holding back.

An arm's length away, Ferrier shoved her hands under her legs and rocked a little side to side. "Your Nan's spells are what allowed us to build this fort. Her magic doesn't need continuous energy."

I nodded at her, grateful that I didn't have to look at Ash. I was certain he could feel my thundering pulse.

"But it's probably also how this Labyrinth was built in the first place," Ferrier rambled on. "Otherwise, the amount of energy needed to keep it up and running would have destroyed the master of this place."

At her words, I locked eyes with Ash, but neither of us spoke. It seemed none of them knew the truth, which meant Ash hadn't given them his full name.

Only I knew that we sat with the man who built this prison and whose actions outlawed our magic. He stared at me, perhaps waiting to see if I would reveal his secret. For some reason, my lips remained pressed shut.

Ash released my hand.

"Done," he said. "You should put some of this on your other wounds." He set the tin beside me.

An unexpected emptiness filled me as he backed away and stood. When he felt me staring, his eyes flashed to mine, and I blinked, feeling foolish. The heightened danger of this place was messing with my rationality and emotions. That was all. In a survival situation, people helped each other. It didn't mean anything.

Except that my heart was all fluttery as he gripped one of the ropes hanging from an upper branch and slipped down, out of sight.

He was the villain in all the history books, the one who broke the world. And he was nothing like I'd imagined.

I grabbed the tin of healing ointment and dabbed the cool salve on my feet and the scratches from the thorns. My heart clenched in my chest as I thought of my brothers. Even with Nan here, and these kind strangers, I still burned with a desire to escape, to protect my brothers—though only one of them was capable of manifesting magic—from the eyes of the king. If anything, discovering Nan was still alive fueled my yearning to be free.

I looked up at Ferrier. "Have you ever tried to escape this place?"

Ferrier jumped at the sudden question. Her slightly rounded face shook quickly. "No. You'll die."

"What?"

Her eyes widened. "If you try, you die. Everyone here knows that."

"What about digging?"

"Buried alive."

"Swimming?"

Another head shake. "Anything you can think of, someone has tried it." Her expression looked too sad in that moment to be on such a young face.

Her words settled heavily on me. The mist had a mostly silver tint to it now, but the blue eddies of fog writhed around the clearing below like a pool of angry snakes.

For several moments, neither of us spoke. My hand gradually numbed, thanks to the healing salve, and the tension in my muscles drained, leaving me so sluggish I could barely turn my head. My body had been in near-constant terror since I arrived, and this moment of respite was dragging me down into what was to be a deep sleep. As the sounds of a fresh, crackling fire drifted up to the treehouse platform, I couldn't hold off the exhaustion any longer. I only hoped no monsters attacked while I slept.

9

The scent of grilled meat roused me from my nightmare. I sat forward, hands splayed on the wooden platform beside me. My abdomen smarted, and I touched the torn fabric darkened by dried blood. The pain had been mitigated by the magical ointment, but the wounds still throbbed gently.

Glancing around for my companions, I noted the décor of this treehouse, something that had slipped past me earlier, when I'd been in such a nervous state. The platform had three levels, each only a step apart, situated around the largest branches of the enormous tree. The middle level where Nan slept was partitioned off with a strip of fabric that hung from an overhead branch. The highest level, which curved around to the opposite side of the tree, also had a makeshift curtain serving as a wall, which hindered my view of it, as did the massive trunk. Ash's quiver of arrows hung on the broken stump of a sawn-off limb. A pair of women's white undergarments spread over another branch. The contrast between the two items elicited a nervous giggle from my chapped lips.

"You awake up there?" Edith called.

I leaned over the edge of the lowest platform, gripping the sides with all my might. Down below I spotted a crackling fire a few paces from the tree. Edith sat with her hands cupped around a steaming bowl. Ferrier paced around the edge of the small clearing, her booted feet so quiet, I could barely hear a dead leaf crackling.

Ash leaned against the tree, directly below me. As he rolled his head up, he locked eyes with me, and a wave of unexpected nerves danced down my skin. Silly me. I was in a death trap with mind mages. There was no time for butterflies from handsome boys...even boys who'd saved my life.

I had to remember who he was. What he'd done.

You can choose to believe what the king's version of history told you about me. His words echoed in my mind. Had the king lied about his enemy? The king was *my* enemy now, so was it so farfetched to believe he'd twisted the truth? Maybe this place was merely messing with my head. After all, Edith warned me of the Labyrinth's lies.

I shifted back and swung my legs over the side of the platform, likely only as high as twice my body length, willing my heart not to fall out of my chest as my feet dangled over the ground. I'd run from an enchanted, murderous moose. This platform shouldn't leave me shaking so badly.

Sensing my hesitation, Edith called up, "Stay there. I've got something for you."

My bare feet slithered back onto the platform, and I tucked them under my crossed legs.

Edith set her bowl down and wiped her hands on her sides. "We found fresh clothing. Let me show you."

She rose, picking up a dress that was draped over a log beside the crackling fire. When she moved, I saw a wash bowl along with other items of clothing that were scattered over rocks and stumps near the fire to dry.

Within seconds, the rope was shaking. Edith scampered up it like a lizard on a brick wall.

"Feeling better?" she asked as soon as she was on the platform.

I nodded.

"Excellent. I think Ferrier slept for two straight days when we arrived. I was forced to carry her." Shadows ghosted Edith's features, as if memories plagued her mind. "Fear is exhausting."

I made a throaty noise of agreement, but I hated to think that it was merely fear that pressed my body down like a thousand stones laid across my chest.

"How long did I sleep?"

"A full day. We decided to let you sleep."

My eyes bulged a little. The twilight falling around us meant I'd missed an entire night and the following day.

"And no monsters came while I slept?"

"Oh, one did," Edith said, a little too nonchalantly, pulling the extra dress from around her neck, where she'd draped it to climb the rope. "Giant snake this time."

My heart seized up a moment.

"Fortunately, Nan's spells can't break, and Ash stuck around. He's almost *too* good at killing the monsters. He hasn't stayed this long in...well, since we built this place. He's usually in and out, bringing something we need, then gone again."

Edith's eyes bored into me, like she was trying to pry out hidden information. Did she think Ash had stayed for me? The idea made my cheeks flush, but I shook the preposterous thought away. He'd gotten me safely to the fort, so why had he stayed?

Edith held out the dress. "The Labyrinth hath provided."

I took the clean, simple, homespun dress and clutched it to my chest. "I can finally get out of this wretched wedding dress. Where'd you find this, anyway?"

Edith shrugged. "We search for food or water, herbs or knives, or what have you. We find what we need, so long as we don't succumb to the fear. Sometimes it takes a day or two, but we always find it." She leveled a warning look at me. "But whatever items this place gives, it's taken them from someone else. At least we can say the Labyrinth doesn't waste. And the person who wore that clearly didn't last long, given how few rips are in it."

My hands released the dress. I wanted to scoot out from under it, but I was already too close to the platform's edge.

Edith picked up the dress. "It's just the way of things here. When someone dies, the Labyrinth sends the valuable items to the next worthy person. There's a sentience here, and it scares me to my bones." She held the dress out, and I took it back more reluctantly. "Don't worry, I washed it. And it's mostly dry already. Every time the Labyrinth helps, it's only drawing us in, making us think we can trust it." She shook her head violently. "Never trust it. Take the dress. Be thankful for it. But never—never—think this maze is on your side."

Ash stoked the fire below, which hissed and snapped. Fresh waves of delightful smelling meat rose into the air. My heart tripped as I caught sight of him. Edith was right, Ash wasn't on my side. I couldn't let his actions change what I knew to be true of him.

Edith moved toward the middle level. "Up here, honey," she said, pulling back the makeshift curtain to reveal Nan, sitting upright and reading a tiny book in the light of a glowing orb that hovered over her head. I'd only seen that kind of magical light in one other place: outside the Guild. My eyes widened, impressed.

Nan smiled at me, and the weight in my chest lessened.

Forcing myself not to look down, I crawled onto the higher level. The makeshift curtain fell, and I knew no one from below could watch me changing clothes.

"I'm glad you were able to sleep so long," Nan said, setting her book aside.

Edith helped me out of the tattered lace dress, clicking her tongue at the sight of the reddened puncture wounds on my stomach and leg. She slipped behind the curtain to retrieve the tin of healing ointment, which she reported was now down by the fire—Ash had needed it after battling the large snake.

"How did you get a *book*?" I asked once Edith left.

She lovingly pressed her hands to the sides of the small book. "I brought it with me."

"They let you keep it?" I settled down beside Nan.

"They didn't know I had it. Their spells couldn't detect the locked spell I'd used to conceal this in the folds of my dress."

I smirked at Nan. "You're full of surprises."

"And so are you." Her large knuckles twitched back and forth over the edge of the book. Her constant little twitches and shakes were so familiar, so comforting. "I think he knows you're a key, or suspects it."

I hugged my arms around my chest, not needing to ask who she meant. "He knows," I whispered. "It's why he brought me here, so I could learn to control my magic—magic I didn't even know I was doing. But he said he would leave once he brought me here safely." By now I was fairly certain Nan's mental state could handle the truth about Ash, and I was bursting to tell her, so I leaned over and whispered, "Did he ever tell you his full name?"

Before Nan had a chance to respond, however, the rope wriggled, indicating Edith was on her way back up. The truth about Ash would have to wait. Edith scrambled onto the platform and hurried to my side, carrying the tin of healing ointment. I took the ointment with a smile, shimmied out of the sleeves of the dress once more, and dabbed the salve onto my wounds.

When I finished, my wounds were cool from the healing ointment, and I felt cleaner than if I'd just climbed out of a hot bath. But I couldn't stop rubbing my hands down the dress, as if I could rub away the knowledge that this dress had recently been on a dead woman. I was alive, and my very alive body was now in this dress.

Would this dress soon be worn by yet another?

I shook off the awful thought and followed Edith to the edge of the platform, where I could see Ash eating a hunk of meat with his bare hands.

"Food's ready," Edith said over her shoulder to Nan. "I'll bring you some."

Edith lowered herself down the rope, then looked up at me. "Your turn."

Ferrier still walked the perimeter of the small clearing, her steps so measured and neat that I wondered if she was under some enchantment. Ash was scrubbing something in the wash bowl, his back to us. He and Edith exchanged a few words, then he glanced up at me. His shirt...that's what he was washing. His vest was open over his bare chest. His eyes caught the firelight and blazed like twin sparks in the deep shadows of the misty forest, ghoulish in their contrast to his darkened features. Edith grabbed a small parcel from near the fire and hurried back to the tree.

I tore my gaze from Ash's strong arms and peered in terror at the ground below.

"Well? Are you coming down to eat?"

I briefly considered asking her to bring me food so I could eat on the platform, but that sounded pathetic—besides, I desperately needed to relieve myself—so with a huff of determination,

I grabbed the rope. My puncture wound had closed up, thanks to the healing ointment, but it was still sore. My palm smarted against the rough twine, and I yanked my hand back.

Edith motioned to Ash. "Help her down."

He threw something into the fire and stood, wiping his hands on the shirt still in the wash bowl, then moved to stand against the tree, one palm uplifted.

"Here," his gravelly voice came from below. "Throw your feet over. I'll guide you down."

Fortunately, he couldn't see me mouth the word *What?* or the color filling my cheeks.

I didn't have much of a choice. I sank to my knees, shimmied backward, cast a prayer like a fishing line to heaven, and lowered my feet over the side. A warm hand encircled my entire bare foot. I trusted him with my weight, trying very hard not to think of the view he was getting. When I was mostly standing in his hands, I grabbed the rope with my uninjured palm and let him lower me down.

He bent to release my foot when I only had a short distance left to drop, but my one-handed descent ended with a clumsy jolt, and I wobbled against the rope. He reached out and steadied my waist, rendering me momentarily mute.

I whirled around, intending to thank him for his help, but I was met with a closeup view of his chest.

Below his collarbone was a raised scar.

I couldn't take a deep enough breath.

Ash stepped away, pulling his gaze from me while the memory of his hand around my foot burned like a brand into my memory.

He silently resumed washing out his shirt. I imagined the entire maze could hear my heartbeat as I watched him. On battered feet, I gingerly stepped far enough away to take care of my needs in private, hoping no monsters chose that moment to attack. Then I hurried back to the clearing, my appetite leading me to a wooden bowl near the fire stacked with small pieces of grilled meat. Ash raised a brow when my stomach let out a loud gurgling sound.

The meat was leathery and the most delicious thing I'd ever tasted—if scarfing can even be considered tasting. When Ash stood to wring out his shirt, he tossed me an amused look, as if my barbaric eating habits were comical. A laugh burst from my mouth, half-crazed and half-delirious. It felt good to laugh. Ash's resulting smile surprised me, and my stomach flipped over. Attempting to hide my flash of nerves, I spun away, trying to make it look like I was concealing my wolfish manners.

"You can't hide from me," he said. His tone was light, but my blood froze.

He was teasing, surely, but given our present location and his identity, the joke shook me to my core.

Though I was good at hiding my deepest emotions and strongest fears, my surface level reactions always popped right out like oil from a hot pan. My entire body stiffened, and I nearly choked on my piece of meat. Over the steady crackling of the fire, I heard Edith and Nan exchanging a few muffled words up in the fort. Ferrier still marched around in circles, her eyes never straying toward us.

I desperately wanted to fill this heavy silence, so I said the first thing that came to my mind. "Edith said you fought a big snake?"

It sounded so dumb, I cringed internally.

Ash picked up a shirt hanging over a rock and replaced it with his recently washed one. "I couldn't risk you getting hurt, not until I see that you've learned to master your magic." Then to my shock, he removed his vest—affording me a view that would have distracted me from any monster—and pulled his clean shirt down over his head.

I didn't rip my stare away fast enough when he tossed his hair back and looked at me.

"Vera, there's no point."

His voice was low, meant only for me, and my chest caved in at his words. Of course there was no point in looking at him like he was beautiful. He was *him* and we were in *here*.

Defiantly, and with more boldness than I ever had outside the Labyrinth, I locked eyes with him. "I'm not resigned to living out a miserable existence running from your monsters. I'm going to find a way out."

Edith was descending from the platform, and my pulse picked up speed.

Ash scoffed at my declaration. "I might have made them," he spat, "but they aren't mine. I've spent decades trying to keep them away from people, to atone for what I did in the war, though I know I never can." Before I could retort, he'd crossed the distance between us. "I know you won't believe me, but I'm not who I was eighty years ago."

Edith dropped to the ground and stared at us for a moment before walking closer. Ash raked a hand through his hair and turned to place more wood on the fire.

My gaze snapped back to Ferrier, still marching in her little circle. "What is she doing?"

"She's practicing something Nan taught her," Edith replied. "She's determined to prove she's a lock, too, but I don't think she is."

I stared at the young girl walking with a resolute but unfixed expression on her face. "How common is it to be a lock?"

Edith sighed. "Pretty rare. There aren't many mind mages to begin with, and I'd never met a lock before your grandmother."

Ash tossed his vest in the washbowl, and it landed with a splat that made me jump. Every unexpected sound had my nerves dancing on a razor's edge. I sensed something was about to rip me from the imagined comfort of this moment, and soon.

Edith settled on a log by the fire and ate. "Ferrier manifested pretty young, which makes her think she's super powerful." Edith rolled her eyes, but a hint of pride shone on her face. "Right now, she's attempting to lock a spell in place, the way your Nan can. I believe she's trying to control that tree over there, same way Nan controls the one with the fort." She pointed to one a few steps away.

My lips parted in a confused frown. "You can stop the trees from...misbehaving?"

"Someone enchanted them to misbehave in the first place," she quipped. "Whole place is built and maintained by magic, and with a little intervention, we can stay safe enough to survive." She tapped the side of her head.

I couldn't keep my gaze from wandering to Ash, but he ignored me.

Nan had rarely spoken of her magic, and at school, they only told us all the awful things about mind mages. I'd never even imagined mental magic could influence nature. All I knew about mind mages was their ability to control someone else by taking over their thoughts. Architects could build almost anything *with* nature, but I'd never heard of controlling nature. Though a tree enchanted by magic was hardly natural to begin with.

"So she's controlling the magic of this place, not really the tree, right?"

Ash glanced up from his washing as Edith tilted her head back and forth in a noncommittal response.

"Sort of," Edith answered. "We can place enchantments of our own on, say, a tree. When I do it, I'm just adding my magic to the magic that's already here. I'm not able to dismantle the Labyrinth's magic. No one can do that. Nan's spells are so powerful because she can lock them in place and stop thinking about them. The magic of the Labyrinth is technically still in place, but her spell is locked around it."

I didn't miss that Ash exhaled at her words. He might have helped us all in one way or another, but perhaps he wasn't helping as much as he could, despite his claims that he had spells in place to keep people safe.

But he'd fought off a snake to keep us safe. And he'd carried me as we outran a demented moose. The king's version of Henry Asher was starting to sound more and more like a lie.

Edith brushed her hands together and flashed me a smile. "If you're going to be part of this team, it's time we know what you can do."

My lips pinched inward, and my eyes averted. "I don't know any magic."

Edith's smile held, but it bled enthusiasm until it transformed into a frightening grimace. "None at all?"

I shook my head. "I can shut down my pain and emotions pretty well, but I don't think repression is really what you were hoping for."

"Not exactly," Edith said, twisting her mouth to one side.

She sat for a moment, her hands in her lap. Neither of us looked at the other. All the feelings of worthlessness and rejection and shame bubbled up inside, replacing my fear of death and dismemberment with a single resounding worry: that this ragtag crew would also deem me valueless.

The words I hated yet clung to for the excuse they provided fell from my lips. "I'm only a quarter mage." My eyes flashed up to the platform where Nan rested. She'd told me I was a key—whatever that meant—but what did it matter if I was only a quarter mage with fitful magic?

After a long, miserable silence, in which I imagined Edith rehearsing the words to dismiss herself and her sister from my company, Ash turned toward me and said, "You were thrown in here for a reason—because you possess magic the king wants eliminated from his kingdom."

I pinched my eyes closed as a fresh wave of concern for my brothers pricked at my heart.

"And if the king believes you're dangerous," Edith chimed in, "then *I* believe you're dangerous too. In the best way." Her smile had caught fire again and was blazing in her freckled cheeks. "I'll teach you."

"*We* will teach you," Ash echoed, his brown eyes sparking with the reflection of the fire. "But we don't have long. The monsters are coming."

10

My heart tripped and *thunked* against my breastbone as excitement and fear wrestled inside me. "Thank you," I muttered, "but I've never been able to do magic on demand."

"Nonsense," Edith declared, hurrying toward me. "He's right, you know. The Labyrinth will sense what we're doing, and it will come at us. At *you*, especially. It doesn't want you to learn how to fight back. This place thinks like a villain, and it never lets us win for very long."

"Great." I swallowed, sensing Ash's eyes on me. This time, I forced myself not to look at him.

Edith crossed her arms. "Just long enough to let us feel like we *might* have a chance. Then it catches us when we're off guard."

This stolen moment of peace around the fire had lured me into a state of relaxation. I didn't want it to end. Darkness was falling, and I couldn't help but fear the shadows.

Ash added a log to the fire. "One thing you need to remember is that the Labyrinth always lies. Things that appear good—a berry, a stream, a soft place to sleep—they're a trap as often as they're a blessing. This place was built to drive you mad." He cleared his throat. "The walls and landmarks move just when you think you know where they should be."

I nodded, unsure what to make of his statement. Curious how he'd respond, I said, "Whoever built this place must have been truly wicked."

He coughed and poked the fire with a stick. "And builders always obey an architect." He stood and pinned me with a hard glare. The firelight danced on his skin, and for a moment, I couldn't look away.

Edith combed her fingers through her hair, awkwardly not looking at either of us. "The Labyrinth trapped me in a locked room once. For two days. Each minute, the room shrank around me. I was hungry and cold and scared out of my mind, worried to death about my sister. When the walls were so narrow I could barely breathe, I sent out all my magic toward Ferrier, to help her in any way I could. As soon as my thoughts turned from myself, the walls fell away. I was free." She looked over at her sister, who was still pacing. "At least, free from that particular test."

A shudder surged through me. "That sounds awful."

She nodded. "It was. But I learned something valuable. I learned that reality here is malleable. Like a dream we can direct, if we can remain lucid. It's not easy, but it *is* possible with our magic. That gave me hope."

Ash rubbed his beard absently with this thumb, and I wished I could discover what he was thinking. I didn't know him at all, only that he'd saved my life and also considered ending it.

This was all very terrifying and enlightening, but I was in no position to fight back against the Labyrinth. If anything, their declarations only increased my fears. I'd never be able to use magic to fight the madness of this place.

"But enough of that." Edith waved a hand. "You said you don't know how to use your magic. Let me see." She tapped her lips with one finger. "It's been a while since my first lessons, but I remember Ferrier's well enough. My mother taught us both, but she made me help Ferrier when she was too busy. We started with simple experiments, like making each other say a single word."

My lips curled into a cringe. *Forcing* someone to do anything didn't feel the least bit simple.

Edith tilted her head sideways, appraising me with a look of disapproval. "You've grown up hating mind magic, haven't you?"

I cast my eyes down and bit my lip.

"Well, I can tell you that hating it is one reason it never came easily for you. It's like trying to become a gardener while hating the dirt. Doesn't work like that." She straightened up. "If you can push away your condescension and give this a try, we might be able to teach you something that could save your life."

Heat blazed in my cheeks. I'd never meant to offend Edith, and Ash was now eyeing me with a somewhat amused expression partly hidden beneath his beard. I thought about snapping back at them. The *possibility* of mind magic in my blood had caused me to be ostracized my entire life, degraded by my schoolmates, and disdained by my own mother. I wasn't accepted in the magical academy, where true mages could thrive. I wasn't even accepted in my own family. At least, not by my mother. Without my brothers, I'd have gone insane a long time ago.

I'd been trapped in a maze my entire life, running from who I really was.

My frustrations must have been playing like stage actors on my face, because when I glanced back up at Edith and Ash, both were staring at me with greater concern, as if they had heard all my thoughts.

To give myself a reason to look elsewhere, I moved to sit on one of the logs beside the fire. Even with the healing ointment working quickly, my bruised and battered feet still hurt and I was tired of standing on them.

Edith tossed Ash another look, then followed me and squatted to her ankles. "You've got to stop thinking of your magic as an evil thing." She put a hand on my shoulder. "To learn anything about your abilities, you need to *want* to. Mind magic, unlike the other disciplines, isn't just about memorizing a list of enchantments. It requires the entire mind, including your emotions."

Her hazel eyes held genuine concern, but I recalled Ash's words. Nothing here could be trusted. How was I supposed to shift my entire worldview based on the words of someone inside a maze designed to break my mind apart?

Then again, Ash had given me a weapon, and Edith's magic had pulled the thorny vines off of me. If I couldn't trust them, I'd be entirely alone in this maze. The tiny worm of doubt wiggled deep within my consciousness, but I chose to ignore it. Madness was refusing help when it was offered.

I nodded. "All right. I'm ready to try."

"Excellent." She stood and marched several steps away. "When you look at that tree over there, can you *feel* the magic in it?"

Eager to answer with *yes*, I turned toward the tree she indicated, which was neither the tree that held the platform nor the one Ferrier was trying to enchant. I stared at the knobby bark and knit my brow. What was I supposed to see? The mist curled around the trunk in a neat spiral, as if mocking me.

"Do you feel the way the magic fills the tree?"

I schooled my expression before I made an ugly face again. "What does it feel like?"

Edith grunted a little, and my insides constricted. Of course I was bad at this. I was a quarter mage with no experience.

"It just *feels*. Like energy. Like control in your mind. Like a sharp spearmint scent in your nose. It's like...I don't know." Edith dropped her head. "I'm terrible at this."

She glanced at Ash for help, but he was staring into the forest, which made my skin prickle. I sensed it too—we didn't have long.

"When I seek to control the tree," she continued, "I harness my magic—which is a bit like inhaling deeply—and pour it all toward the magic controlling that single tree. I feel it when the magics have connected, and I imagine what I want the tree to do, or rather not do. Keeping something still takes less energy than making something move. Until my control breaks, the tree is unable to move."

My lips pursed and turned down. About ten things in that statement made no sense. But one thing rang a bell. My mind flashed to the woman who'd thrown me in here. She'd appeared to be exhausting herself by forcing me to move as she desired.

"At my wedding—*would be* wedding—I was taken by a woman who worked for the king. She used her magic to force my entire body to move."

Edith nodded. "She probably spent the next day recovering. Those kinds of enchantments take extreme control and use up a lot of energy. As much as he claims to hate us, the king likes to employ a few of us—the most powerful ones—to act like puppeteers, forcing others to do anything the king desires. Comes in handy for a monarch."

Ash grunted. "He likely blackmails them to work for him in the first place."

Edith blinked as if surprised he was listening. "I'm no good at teaching. Ash, you say something."

He snapped out of his thoughts and looked first at Edith, then at me. His chest expanded but no words came out as he held his breath for a moment. Finally, he looked back at Edith and spoke quietly. "If I teach her, we'll have less time."

Edith crossed her arms again. Then a moment later flung them both out at her sides. "Fine." She stomped toward me. "The Labyrinth responds to him more than the rest of us. He can find what we need faster than I ever can, but he draws out the worst monsters. It's like this place hates him the most, because it tries really hard to push him over the edge. You don't ever want to be near him when the Labyrinth decides it's time for his next test."

I nearly choked on my next breath. An owl hooted in the distance.

Edith's gaze lingered on Ash, with a hint of fear. Perhaps his extended presence here endangered her and her sister more than usual? She closed her eyes and remained silent for so long that I wondered if she would be teaching me anything at all. The only sounds were Ferrier's soft steps and the breeze that howled gently in the trees above. The mist continued to whorl and eddy in its own little labyrinthine patterns.

"I was able to resist my captor when I was under her control," I offered, eager to prove myself capable of magic.

Ash's eyes narrowed as he studied me. "She could try to resist your control," he suggested.

Edith pursed her lips, as if that were a pointless suggestion.

A flush entered my cheeks. "Is that not easy to do?"

Edith sat beside me. "No, it's not. And it's not comfortable for the one you're resisting. But, okay, let's try it. I'm going to enter *your* mind and make you raise your arm. Try to stop me."

Faster than I'd anticipated, my arm shot up. I gasped and Edith clapped a hand over her sudden laughter. I chuckled, too, even though a slice of anger carved through my ribcage. But watching her laugh infected me with mirth. Soon, both of us were bent over with laughter that felt better than any healing ointment in the world.

Ash ruined it when he said, "This could save your life, Vera. You should take it seriously."

Years of living with brothers caused me to make a face up at him before I'd realized it might not be the best thing to do in the moment. His brows lifted, but he looked more amused than angry.

"Okay, try again," I said to Edith.

This time, I felt the magic stitching itself into my thoughts. I yanked my arm back and away, but the magic poked harder and soon my arm was above my head again.

"I felt something that time."

Edith clapped. "That's good!"

She let my arm fall back down.

Ash grunted and crossed his arms.

"I'm trying, okay?" I barked at him.

He said nothing.

Edith and I tried several more times. Each time, I could detect when her magic slithered into my own mind, but I still always failed to prevent her from moving my arm. After the sixth time, I shouted in anger and clenched my fists. Instantly, the cuts on my feet burned, and I could no longer sit here and ignore the pain.

I pulled one of my feet up to look at the battered skin. The ointment was helping, but not fast enough. If we had to run again, I'd be hobbling instead.

"That looks bad," Edith admitted, making a face at my up-lifted foot. "Ash, can't you do something?"

My eyes wandered to him, curious about what he could do for my feet.

Edith read my curiosity. "If he walks that way for fifteen minutes, the Labyrinth might just toss him a pair of shoes. It's unfair how easy it is for him."

Ash huffed quietly through his nose, as if he thought *easy* wasn't the best word for it.

"But we can't risk it," Edith concluded, offering me a com-passionate frown. "I imagine the Labyrinth wants to test your pain tolerance. It does that to each of us."

The punctures on my feet had closed, but the soft skin had purpled in several places from my unfortunate encounters with rocks. The ointment only seemed to work on the superficial wounds. The bruises still ached when I walked. Looking at my feet made it harder to ignore the pain, so I tucked my feet back beneath my newly acquired dress.

"You won't be able to run very fast with bruises like that," Edith commented.

"I...I'm pretty good at ignoring pain. I just pretend I'm shut-ting it away in a locked room."

Ash spun toward me quickly, but I missed whatever expression was on his face because I was distracted by Edith clapping merrily.

"Vera, that's magic! You *can* do magic!"

My heart beat so hard between my ribs that I clutched my hands at my chest and leaned forward, head spinning. "I've been doing *magic* without knowing it?"

Before I could ask how all this worked, Ash shot a silencing finger up at us. I froze.

Edith inhaled sharply and leaped up, her eyes scanning the forest.

Ash scurried to the fire and stomped out the embers. In a breath, his knife was in his hand. I hadn't even gotten to my feet.

"Get to the tree," he demanded.

As I started to hobble toward the treehouse, Edith raced to her sister, yanking her from her trancelike march and shoving her toward the fort.

They reached the ropes before I did. I waited, knees bouncing, while the two sisters shimmied up to safety.

On the wind, the faint sound of howling chilled my blood. I glanced back at Ash.

He was backing toward me, knife at the ready for whatever came out of the woods. I stretched out my hand to prevent him from bumping into me.

At my touch, he whirled around, eyes wild. "Up!"

Edith and Ferrier had reached the platform. I grabbed a rope and tried to climb. Ash was up his rope in the time it took me to wrap the wriggling rope around my ankle. I should have practiced rope climbing rather than magic.

"Vera! Climb!" Ash shouted.

Edith yelled something, too, but the howls drowned out all other sounds.

Dark shapes burst from the shadows into the clearing, but I didn't spare them a glance. I flung myself desperately at the rope, ignoring the pain as my wound reopened in my palm. Blood slicked under my grip and my arms shook.

A snout snapped at my ankles, and I screamed.

With a thud, Ash slammed to the ground beside me, knife flashing. A whimpering sound followed by a wicked snarl sent my heart rate soaring. Edith heaved from above as I struggled to use my feet to lift my weight out of my hands.

Something entered my mind then. A snag, a little hook. I was too panicked to try to resist it. But as soon as it settled in my mind, I found myself scaling the rope with ease. As if I'd always known how to do this.

I flopped onto the platform and rolled away from the edge. Edith heaved from her effort, and Ferrier sat with hands clapped over her mouth.

Lying flat against the boards, I stared up at the rustling leaves and swirling mist. The awful snarls from below threatened to choke me as I tried to calm my rapid breathing. Ash could die because of me.

"Oh!"

At Edith's exclamation, I rolled over onto my stomach, catching sight of Ash's hands as they rose into view. He climbed up high enough to drop onto the platform, shaking the structure and rattling a small yelp from my lips. He was alive.

Then I pressed the back of my hand to my open mouth, reeling with the knowledge that I *wanted* him to be alive. No matter what the history books and legends had told me, my heart somersaulted at the sight of him sinking to his knees beside me.

His forearm was bleeding. The magic controlling my mind released and slithered away, but as it left me, the mental image of Ash wrapping his arms around me filled my senses—and it wasn't from my point of view, but from *his*. He looked away quickly.

I stared at him, aware that it was his magic that had controlled me and allowed me to climb the rope to safety. The blue mist appeared to sink into him as the chaos of the barking from below subsided.

Ash remained mostly silent the rest of the evening, avoiding my eyes and sitting as far from me as possible on the platform as Edith and Ferrier asked me about my home and told me of theirs. Nan even moved down to the lower platform, with Ash's help, to join our conversation, adding in bits about my mother and brothers that eventually calmed my knotted nerves. Though I enjoyed the talk of home, I couldn't help but revisit the image I'd received from Ash. Of his arms holding me. Of the way he'd crushed me to his chest.

He'd said there was no point in me looking at him. But now I couldn't possibly stop looking at him. Now, more than ever, I wanted to know the truth about him.

Later, as I stretched out to sleep on the broad lower level of the platform—the only place there was enough room for me—I rolled my head to the side and peered over at Ash, who sat against the trunk, merely an arm's length away.

His wrists rested on his bent knees and his head was tilted back against the bark. He must have felt me staring because he dropped his gaze and met mine.

I tucked my hands under my head and tried not to think of the fact that I was going to have to sleep so close to him.

"Tomorrow, I must go," he muttered, voice low enough that I assumed he only meant for me to hear him.

It felt like someone had sawn a little hole in the platform, and I was tumbling to the ground.

I sat up. "Why?"

"I shouldn't have stayed here so long." His throat bobbed.

After a moment, I said, "Thank you. For saving me earlier."

"I'm sorry you saw what you did. It was foolish of me to think of such things with our minds still connected. Foolish of me to think it at all." He looked away.

I didn't know what he believed, what his past contained, what he enjoyed, what his worst habits were. But I couldn't stop the way my heart seized at his words. Foolish or not, I didn't care anymore.

I scooted forward so I didn't have to whisper so loudly. "I want to know the truth about the war, about you, about all of it."

He shook his head. "I locked most of those memories away. You unlocked some of them a couple of days ago. I'd rather not revisit them."

"Fine. Then tell me something about yourself."

He locked eyes with me. The only light came from the faintly glowing mist and the distant moonlight behind the leaves. "It isn't wise."

I pursed my lips before responding. "You want me to trust you, but you won't let me get to know you? You say you're not the man the king told us all about. Then tell me who you are."

He held my gaze so long that I had to physically restrain myself from crumbling under the weight of it.

"Vera, I may not be the monster you learned about, but I'm no savior. I'll leave tomorrow, and you can learn all you need from Edith."

My heart cracked a little. I'd known him a grand total of a few days—I didn't count the one I'd slept through—but he'd already saved my life more than once. Certainly that made up for time. "I'm not staying in here. I'm going to escape, and you can too."

"Stop talking about escape."

"Why? What's wrong with hope?"

"It's madness."

My gaze narrowed. "I have brothers. I can't leave them to the king's whims."

He rubbed his hand down his face. "You should get some sleep."

I scoffed and hugged my knees, not ready to end this conversation. "Tell me one thing about yourself."

He rolled his eyes. "Edith and your Nan can teach you how to control your magic. You'll be safe here with them."

"As a kid, I always wanted a treehouse," I said. "I guess I've got one now."

His lips twitched, but he didn't respond.

"Now you tell me something."

He sighed. "Vera, go to sleep."

"One thing. Just tell me one thing."

"Fine," he huffed, raking a hand through his hair. "I always wanted to become a professor."

My face lit with a smile. "Like at the university?"

He nodded. "I wanted to teach mathematics." He shook his head. "Useless dream."

"No," I blurted, a little too loudly. I flinched and quieted my voice. "It's a great dream."

"The only dream I have now is to help as many people survive their first day in here as I can. But the madness takes them all, eventually." He stood, stepped to the other side of the platform, which wasn't very far, and lay down. He never glanced back my way, and within a few seconds, his deep breathing indicated he was already asleep.

That night, I dreamed of Ash running through the Labyrinth in a professor's robe—but as he ran, the robe reached up and wrapped around his throat, choking him.

11

Ash kept his word and left the following day.

An unexpected hollowness formed in his absence. I'd slept easier with him nearby, but after two more days living in constant fear of another attack, I once again fell asleep quickly.

"If the Labyrinth is pleased with him leaving us, we might even have a day or two of rest," Edith said on the second day after Ash's departure.

Her words provided little comfort.

I found that the routine of waking, finding food and water, practicing magic, and sleeping became a rhythm that kept the fear at bay. But each day that Ash did not reappear, dread pooled in my gut. I couldn't stop my mind from reinventing the way his hands had doctored my wound or steadied me when I'd come down the rope. Perhaps it was the adrenaline surging in my veins at all times, but in such a short time, he'd burned his place in my memory, and there was no forgetting him.

"This time, see if you can stop my control from ever taking root in your mind," Edith suggested as we picked blueberries from a wild bush. These bushes didn't sit in one place, but every day, a fruit-bearing bush or tree would appear somewhere in the Labyrinth, and it was a mad dash to find it before any of the Nameless discovered it. Edith admitted that most days they never found it before having to return to the fort.

I dropped the fat berries into the apron tied to my waist. I'd worn Ferrier's boots today, as we'd been alternating who wore them. My feet were so tiny, though, that even her boots were too large. My feet slipped around inside them, rubbing blisters in several places. But blisters were better than stepping on rocks.

Edith's magic latched onto my mind. I cringed and concentrated on not letting the berries scatter to the grassy forest floor. We were in a small clearing where early morning sunshine lit the sparkling mist, creating a deceptively beautiful scene.

I ground my teeth and pushed against Edith's mental hold, but my moment of distraction trying to save the berries had been enough for her magic to fully sink in. She shared a quick memory with me, of her and Ferrier riding horses through a field of wildflowers. I practiced what Nan had told me, and I pictured the scene dissolving like smoke. According to Nan, I had the ability to stop any spell.

The scene dissipated, and Edith's mental hold relaxed. "I sensed it that time. That was better." She smiled. "I always loved that field in the summertime."

My lips quirked, but instead of smiling, a weight sank in my chest. Her memory was a happy one, but it reminded me of my brothers. Of my goal to escape. "I want to look for the wall again," I admitted.

Edith pinched the edges of her blueberry-laden apron together and glared at me. "Don't start that talk again."

Shoulders sinking, I resigned myself to having to search for a way out on my own, though I hated the idea of leaving my friends. I would wait until my magic was stronger, and then I would go. A few more days. But I would come back for them. For Nan.

My eyes scanned the forest all around. Oddly, now that Ash was gone, every time I glanced about, a mixture of fear and hope filled my lungs as I held my breath, searching for signs of movement.

Perhaps the Labyrinth was finished merging our paths and now was preventing him from returning. Or perhaps it was silly of me to think he wanted to return.

I popped a berry into my mouth, relishing its sweetness.

"Do you hear that?" asked Edith, her eyes wide.

Every muscle in my body tensed.

"There." Edith pointed at a massive shape lumbering through the trees, knocking the large trunks aside like daffodils.

We bolted from the berry bush without a second glance, and I spilled every berry I'd collected onto the ground. Edith shot me one panicked look as she darted into the woods. Rumbling filled the growing darkness, and the ground beneath me shook. Then, before I had taken two steps, a wall shot up from the ground, spewing dirt as it rose. I couldn't follow Edith now.

Whirling back the other direction, I spotted the monster.

Strange, waxlike droplets fell from the beast's skin as it stormed into the clearing. Its face was a marred net of scars but vaguely resembled a bull's with a huge iron ring in its nose. The creature crashed over the open space and swung an arm at me. Where feet should have been, there were hooves. In one hand, the minotaur carried a curved blade.

Without thinking, I shoved my fear aside and leaped into a sprint. My feet seemed to float over the forest floor as I ran for my life. This place had severed me from my companion. The Labyrinth really did have a mind of its own. Soon, I was shrieking as I tried to draw breath. The monster labored toward me, trees and branches snapping as it came.

I couldn't outrun this towering beast. My fear flooded back into my mind and threatened to crack my composure when I stopped and faced the creature, who was only steps away. I gritted my teeth and concentrated on the one thing I had to do: fight back.

My ability to think straight shattered like a dropped clay plate. Panic sent my concentration flying in a hundred directions, and my bodily instinct to survive was all that remained. I drew the knife at my waist and screamed as the beast barreled down on me.

It sidestepped my stabbing motion and swiped at me with its massive arm. I ducked before even thinking. The monster snorted in anger and glared at me with reddish eyes.

I wouldn't survive this if I let fear win. Instead, I quickly pictured a trap door in the forest floor, shoved my fears inside it, and slammed it shut.

The change was instant. My spine straightened. My hands steadied. I narrowed my eyes at the beast that charged me once more.

When I hurled the knife, my aim was true. But the handle only knocked the beast's wide neck and fell to the ground.

An eerie calm flowed through my veins, even though I was now weaponless. I knelt to the ground, one ankle extended, right as the creature's hooves tore past me.

Its foot hooked my leg, and it toppled forward with a loud smash. It writhed for a second, the blue mist pulsing in a frenzy around the monster. The minotaur got to its feet, and in that moment, magic attempted to thread itself into my thoughts.

I slapped the magic away and darted to grab the knife.

The creature turned, rage in its tiny eyes, and lunged into another charge. I bent my knees, ready to sink my dagger into the creature's thigh. Heart in my throat, I screamed as another shape shot out of the forest, taking the monster down in a snarling heap.

A flash of brown vest and blond hair rolled out of view as the monster lurched up from the ground.

"Ash!"

My chest combusted.

He was on his feet in a second. A blade protruded from the monster's back. It faltered, but only barely, before swiping at Ash with an arm as thick as a small tree.

Ash didn't leap aside fast enough. He was thrown against a nearby tree so forcefully that the branches shook.

Think!

I recalled Edith's words about everything here being enchanted. As the beast raced toward Ash, I screamed in anger, picturing myself hooking its nose with a large chain.

The beast's head jerked sideways.

My brows shot up. I tugged on that mental image, drawing the beast away from Ash with nothing more than my mind. I let out a shocked laugh. The minotaur's waxy skin appeared like the edges of a dripping candle, and I shivered with disgust.

Then an idea hit me. I pictured a candle, burned to the bottom of the wick, nothing more than a heap of wax.

The beast snarled, and its body puddled onto the forest floor, sinking quickly out of sight among the leaves.

Stunned, I watched as a few bits of ash floated from the ground where the minotaur had disappeared. They mingled with the glittering mist until I couldn't tell them apart.

It was nearly midday, and silvery mist glistened in the full sunlight. The forest was still. Mist arced in little rivers here and there, as always, coursing through the forest on its own terms. Heart pounding, I searched anxiously for signs of other monsters. Nothing but a hooting owl.

And Ash, who was pushing himself off the ground. He groaned, and my heart collapsed. I wanted to ask if he was all right, but my mind was spinning, teetering on the verge of shock. My pulse had risen to the thrum of a hummingbird's wings, and I felt lightheaded. So instead, I knelt on the forest floor and tried to regain control of my breathing.

His bearded face tightened, but his lips pressed into a small smile. "You didn't need my help." He didn't sound relieved, exactly. Surprised, maybe. It rattled something inside me, like a small pebble dislodging from a mountainside a few minutes before a landslide.

My chest hollowed as I waited for him to speak. He'd made it clear he wouldn't stick around just for me, and yet here he stood.

He carefully rolled both sleeves back up to his elbows. "You're not bad at magic if you can do that."

I shook my head. "I've never been able to do magic like that. I know you don't believe me, but it's true. I've gotten so used to being mocked for my faulty magic that I can't even believe you're complimenting me right now." I lifted my arms. "It feels like you're mocking me."

Ash stepped forward, no longer trying to keep his movements quiet. I staggered to my feet and backed up.

"You destroyed that beast. That's not something most mages can do."

My heel knocked into a wall that hadn't been there a moment ago. I let out a small, *"Oh."*

Ash's eyes traced the wall in both directions, as if puzzled by its appearance as well. "This place is on to you," he muttered, almost growling. "It's not going to stop until you're…" His words stopped, and he ran both hands through his hair, distracting me with a view of his strong arms. "I can't let this place destroy you."

That wasn't what I was expecting.

My recent encounter with the minotaur had left me shaken, and now this. My mouth hung open, words vanishing in my throat before I could voice them.

"And believe me, it would be better for me if I could," Ash continued. His dark eyes reflected the glowing mist, which painted his face with a ghostly silver hue. "You're the only person in this maze who knows who I really am. I assumed you would hate me for who I am, but instead you wanted to *get to know me.*" He smirked. "In eighty years, of all the people who've learned who I am, you're the only one who hasn't run away or tried to kill me, and I can't let you die."

I had hated him, at first, assuming I knew all there was to know about Henry Asher. I still wanted to know the truth about the war, but his words rocked me, and I was unable to speak for several seconds.

Finally, my words surfaced, and I asked the one thing that felt safest. "Was that beast only a spell?"

Ash's cheekbones cast deep shadows as he peered down at me. "Yes and no. It had flesh and bone. But everything in this maze was put here by magic and is sustained by magic. You broke the enchantment that created that monster." He rubbed his neck as if his recent encounter with the tree had left him in pain. "How were you not afraid?"

My blistered feet were throbbing again, and I tried to find the door in my mind where I locked away unpleasant things. I'd inadvertently let the door burst open in the shock of watching the monster vanish, and all my fears had returned. Including the fear of having to watch Ash leave again.

"I shut my fear away. In a little room."

Ash's hands reached for my face so fast I cringed. But his warm, calloused palms held me firmly but gently. I was forced to return his searching stare.

"You shouldn't do that," he warned, eyes wide with worry.

"It's the only way I was calm enough to fight."

His breaths hit my cheeks, and I tingled all over. Then his hands fell away. "I think, Vera Rivers, that you are not at all what you've believed your entire life."

As if this place was designed to destroy everything I believed possible, he dropped to his knees and slipped one hand under the hem of my dress to wrap his fingers around my ankle.

I gulped in a breath so violently that I coughed to recover.

"You've been closing off your pain, too, haven't you? It's your feet, isn't it?"

He lifted my foot, and I lost my balance, my arm shooting out for anything that could steady me. I grabbed a fistful of his hair.

His head jerked up and his eyes met mine.

I loosened my grip but kept my hand on his head, feeling like I might crumple to the forest floor without something to steady me. His eyes blazed, and he didn't look away for an eternal second. Then he slipped off the too-large boot and bent lower to examine the bleeding blisters on my foot. His thumb caressed the skin beside the wound, sending little tingles of warmth through my veins.

My balance now restored, I loosened my fingers and slid them reluctantly out of his hair.

"You don't have to let go," he said, his eyes still down.

I imagined he could feel my pulse hammering under my skin. Although I dreamed of sliding my fingers back into his hair, I tucked my hand carefully against my side instead.

"Still afraid to touch me?" he asked, voice gravelly.

To prove that I wasn't, I slid one hand slowly into his hair. His eyes drifted closed and I nearly lost my ability to breathe.

"If you shut too much of yourself away, it can kill you. Did your Nan tell you that?"

My instinct was to defend Nan, but she had never warned me of this. I answered truthfully. "She never knew how much of myself I needed to shut away."

He released my foot, and his touch traced up my ankle for a split second before he stood. I was breathless when his hand found the back of my neck.

"Whoever taught you that you could be discarded was a fool." His forehead tipped against mine. "There's nothing you need to hide. You're exquisite."

A small, shocked sound escaped my lips.

"Is this okay, Miss Rivers, or do you want me to let you go?"

My fingers tensed on his arm, holding him in place.

Then his mouth met mine, stealing the breath I was trying to take, kissing me like it was dangerous, like he was teetering on madness. I felt it too. Everything inside me seemed to come undone.

When he pulled away, I stared up at him in wonder, my head shaking in disbelief mingled with crazed joy. I'd never felt more whole or more seen than I did in this moment.

I meant to ask *what now*, but I knew what I had to do next. I had to get out. To save my brothers. To have a life where *this* was possible, not in stolen moments between running from monsters. If I was a key, then just maybe there was something I could do to unlock the magic holding us all captive.

"I...should take you back to Edith and Ferrier," he said, a strange ache pinching the corners of his eyes.

I wasn't ready for this moment to break. Even the swirling silver mist seemed to dance in joyful whorls. But I needed to see Nan, to make sure she was all right. To see my new friends. When Ash turned to go, blue fingers of mist reached for him.

"Wait," I breathed.

He turned back toward me, brows lifted.

"Teach me. You said I needed to learn."

His attention shifted, fixing on a nearby tree instead of my face. "You don't need my help."

"I..." *want it*. But I couldn't say that aloud. Instead, I said, "I still don't know what I'm doing."

"If I help you, the Labyrinth won't like it. It's likely already planning to test you again. You've learned too much, achieved too much for it to leave you alone now."

"I just want to survive long enough to get out."

He turned fully toward me now. "You can't beat this place. Don't think you can, just because you discovered your magic. This place wants you... It wants to break you." He swallowed, fear touching the corners of his eyes.

It struck me as odd to see fear on his face. I'd seen him look carefree in the face of monsters. "I didn't think you were afraid of this place."

"I'm not."

"Then what?"

He was breathing faster now. "I'm afraid for you. Afraid you'll be torn to pieces, and I won't be able to stop it. Afraid of what it means that I care for you, and afraid of what will happen when you're gone."

His words hit me like a series of unexpected punches. I couldn't recover fast enough.

"Your magic broke open a part of me I thought was locked forever. And you did it without even trying."

Barely making a sound, I mumbled, "I'm sorry."

His eyes closed, and he grimaced. "It's not your fault. But I see nightmares when I'm around you, Vera. Nightmares I locked away a long time ago."

I blinked. "Nightmares?"

His eyes were sad when they opened again. "The ones I hid because they'll drive me to madness faster than any monster."

The way he'd held a knife at my throat made a little more sense now.

"No one's magic has ever affected me like this. I need it to stop. But I can't leave you alone in this place, because the thought of a monster hurting you, I can't...I won't let that happen."

I watched him turn and walk back the way he'd come. "Ash."

He paused, his shoulders rising and falling with his quick breaths.

There were likely a thousand things I could say—should say in this moment—but I stepped carefully over the fallen leaves, stopped at his side, and said, "Teach me how to fight the monsters, like I did back there, and you won't have to worry. Teach me how to break the spells that control them."

His fingers twitched, and my heart leaped skyward at the idea that he might take my hand.

Instead, he fisted his hand and said, "If you start tearing this place apart...if you start breaking the rules, there will be consequences, and I won't be able to save you from them all."

12

An hour later, Edith and Ferrier jumped up to embrace me when I entered the clearing below their fort.

"You survived!" Ferrier said, smiling broadly.

I glanced at Ash, who hovered at the edge of the clearing with his hands in his pockets. Our gazes locked for a brief moment.

Edith traced the invisible line between me and Ash. "Oh, and I found you a pair of boots. These should fit you better."

I clapped a hand to my face and let out a sigh that sounded too much like a whimper. I dove for the boots, trying to forget that my feet would be comfortable only because someone had died. My mouth twisted at the idea, but my feet rejoiced at the embrace of the leather that didn't rub on the open blisters.

With my boots secured, my attention turned toward the platform in the enormous tree. "Nan," I whispered, stepping over toward the rope.

Already, I'd mastered rope climbing, never wanting to repeat the awful episode with the wolves. I wrapped the rope around my leg and foot, then stepped on it to lift myself. It wasn't graceful, but I eventually rose to the platform and clambered to where Nan lay. She was still, and I held my breath.

When my hand touched her shoulder, she rolled over. She looked tired but glad to see me.

"Vera."

I closed my eyes in relief. That minotaur had rattled me, and her voice felt like a warm blanket tucked around my chilled shoulders.

"You're alive!" I breathed.

Nan twisted around, and I helped prop her against the branch behind her head. "My dear, there are two truths you need to know, and you need to accept them without argument."

I sat back, a little surprised by her forwardness, but eager to listen.

"First, I've set up some fairly secure protections for myself right here. You needn't worry about me. Edith, Ferrier, and Ash have provided everything I need, and in return, I've locked some enchantments in place to help them. Some they know of, others they do not." Her wrinkled face curved in a small smile. "I have helped as many as I can, but my time is running out. I am tired." At my quick gasp, she raised her hand. "Now, mind you, I'm not in any hurry to die. I'm merely finished running. I've made my peace with this place, as much as anyone can. And I'm as comfortable as is likely to be possible in this place."

A wave of emotion swept through me as I recalled Nan's funeral. How I'd wept then, thinking she was gone. A tear pressed into the corner of my eye.

"And second," she continued, her voice firmer and her shoulders stiffening in a way that made me sit up straighter for what she was about to say, "that boy is not who you think he is. For one thing, he is a lock like me. That might be useful information for you." Nan pressed on before I could interject. "And the only other thing I will say—well, there are two things. When the moment comes for you to learn what I know, I want you to remember that he's put himself at great personal risk to help you."

"I know who he is, Nan."

Her gray eyebrows rose. "Oh. I see," she said with a faint smile. "He doesn't even know that I know. But watching someone can tell you a lot about them, especially when you can feel their magic." She leaned forward slightly. "The things the king said about him, not even half of them are true, and those truths have been twisted to fit the king's purposes. Only those alive before the war know this, and most of us are dead now. I was young, but I remember what my father said about Henry Asher." She lifted a hand. "I'm not the one to set the record straight, my dear. He must tell you, and I suspect he will, in time. One other thing, if you care for him—and I suspect you do by the way your magic feels when I talk about him—try to forgive him. People who are afraid or wounded, especially those never given a chance to heal, often hurt others. And I suspect he carries deep wounds."

Visions of my mother grated against my already spinning thoughts. After my father died, she had grown even cold-er—more distant—than she'd been before. Trying to make sense of the turmoil in my head, I pressed my hands against my eyes and commanded myself to calm down.

For a short while, I sat with Nan, as I had each day since I'd arrived at the fort, answering more questions about Archer and Danny and the two years of our lives she'd missed, until she fell asleep once more.

Lying so still, she looked frail. Magic was a strange strength, the kind you couldn't see. It was like love or bravery. My lips curled into a smile as I watched her shallow breaths. She was the strongest person I knew.

Edith and Ferrier had climbed up to the platform while Nan and I were talking. Edith lifted her head when I stepped down from Nan's little room.

"Thank you for taking care of her," I whispered, glancing back up at Nan.

"She's the reason we're still alive." Edith touched her sister's shoulder.

Living in this place with my loved ones, constantly fearing for their lives—that would drive anyone to madness. A renewed respect for Edith settled in my bones.

Ash's dark shape moved around the clearing below, and my heart flipped inside my chest. I clumsily made my way down the rope, dropping when my hands gave out to land with a painful jolt on the uneven ground.

Hands reached out to steady me.

I spun around quickly to face Ash, blood thrumming excitedly in my veins.

Nan's words about him—*he carries deep wounds*—rang in my head. I grabbed the edges of his vest before he could release me.

I whispered, quietly so Edith might not hear, "She knows who you are."

His expression was hard to read in the shadows under the platform, but he gave a small nod. "She's a smart woman."

Ash stepped away, but I kept pace with him as he edged across the clearing.

"Tell me about the war," I said. I didn't care that he had wounds. It only made me more eager to know what they were, to offer him a chance to heal.

He ran a hand down his face. "I took men's lives."

A long breath escaped my lungs. "Like you said, it was war."

"Not every life I took was in defense of a noble cause, Vera. Taking lives leaves a mark. Those I killed with my magic haunted my mind endlessly, until I locked those thoughts away. You broke open those memories."

I cringed as the image of the decimated battlefield flooded my mind. I recalled the strange vision of a woman's face I'd seen another time Ash was near. But I didn't want to ask about her. Not with the memory of his kiss still blazing on my lips. So I said, "Teach me how to control it, so I don't hurt you again."

And if I learned to hone my magic, maybe I could unlock a spell that would finally allow us to escape. But I kept this part to myself, not wanting to give him a reason to say no.

After a long pause, he grumbled, "Not here. The Labyrinth will test you again if it senses you're doing magic. We can't put the others at risk. Follow me."

I trailed Ash through the thick forest, the trees like pale skeletons and the mist a phantom. Every flicker of the writhing fog lifted the hairs on my arms. Edith's words about the Labyrinth turned in my head. *There is sentience here.*

A huge fallen tree up ahead forced us to angle to the right, toward moss-covered stone walls that I hadn't noticed before. The mist thickened, and there was only one way to go: a small space between the walls that appeared like a dark doorway.

"This way," he muttered, ducking through the narrow opening.

We entered an open space surrounded by moss-covered stone walls. The sunlight shone through the trees at an angle, creating pockets of bright light and deep shadow. Perhaps more of the afternoon had passed than I'd realized. Ash paced in the small clearing beside a crumbled stone structure. It might have been an abbey once, with its pointed windows and simple rectangular shape, but there was no ceiling, and the stones, at least those visible under spiderwebs of dead vines, were scorched black. I didn't think any buildings existed in the Labyrinth, but clearly, I was wrong.

With his back still to me, he said, "Everyone experiences magic differently. You might see it, or you might hear it. Some people smell it, like Edith does, and others taste it. Once you determine your lens, it's much easier to focus on the magic."

Part of me wondered why Edith hadn't mentioned this, but I couldn't let myself worry about that now. I had plenty to worry about as it was.

The blood in my veins trilled from a jumble of antagonizing forces: my fear that some monster would emerge from the ground and eat my ankles, my dread that Ash would decide never to kiss me again, and my own quiet terror that I might never escape this place and my brothers would be left to the whims of the king.

I concentrated on Ash's words. I *wasn't* some magicless quarter-mage, but a true mage. A *mind* mage capable of terrible and powerful things. The very thing I'd never wanted to be and yet always secretly hoped to be. And I was a key, capable of dismantling magic few others could, thanks to the blood of my grandmother. All my life, I'd hoped to be like my grandfather—a fire mage. But somehow, now that I knew I had Nan's magic, a feeling of pride welled within me that overpowered the fears trying to steal my focus.

Ash stopped pacing and moved only his eyes toward me. "Still nothing?"

It took me a moment to realize he was asking me a question. I'd been too distracted, both by his jawline and the whispering wind in the trees.

I shook my head.

He sighed. "Then tell me everything you're sensing right now. Any odd colors? Smells? It could even be a breeze or a subtle shadow or maybe heat or a musical sound."

He walked closer as he spoke, until his boots nearly touched mine and he towered over me. Heat flared up my neck, but I schooled my expression. His nearness didn't scare me. Or at least, it shouldn't, and I didn't want him to think I was inexperienced at staring up into the faces of handsome men.

"What do you feel?"

His question prodded me from my temporary stupor. "It's cold."

A half-lie. I was sweating, but the air was cold around me.

"I feel the stone bench behind me, the damp fog around me, the breeze against my skin, and the hunger inside me." I broke away from his intense stare. "I see trees and a crumbling abbey and a misty blue forest. And you. What's so strange about any of that?"

He reached for me, and his thumb grazed my cheek, then he let out a startled, single-note laugh. My heart flipped, and I sucked in a breath.

"Did you say blue mist?"

"It's sort of silvery blue."

He snapped triumphantly. "That's it." He backed away so fast he pulled a cold breeze behind him that tugged at my loose hair. "Vera, there's no mist here."

I glanced around. The forest was covered in it. "But..."

"It's summer. There isn't heavy mist in summer."

"This is the Labyrinth. I assumed anything goes."

He tilted his head back, smiling. His long hair brushed his shoulders, and I was distracted by the point in his throat.

"That's true. But I can assure you, this Labyrinth is not *misty*. That's entirely too predictable, and this place was built to shock and frighten."

Wrapping my hands around my shoulders, I spun in a half circle, turning away from Ash to observe the way the mist swirled and danced, a creature all its own.

My blood chilled and gooseflesh formed down my arms. "All of that is magic?"

His voice was closer when he answered. "Yes."

I didn't turn to face him as my body began to tremble. "All this time, it's been right in front of me. But I've never seen magic before," I admitted, still unable to face him. "Why can I see it here?"

His heat warmed my back—he was so close. I still couldn't fathom why I was attracted to a man I'd grown up reviling, but here we were. Turned out that the childhood nightmares about monsters in the water were more real than the history lessons we'd learned about the war.

"If you've never seen magic before," he said, "then the only explanation is that someone locked an enchantment on you to keep you from seeing it and that the enchantment broke when you entered the Labyrinth. Outside spells can't make it through the door."

Warmth flooded down my spine so suddenly I shuddered. Whirling around to hide my tremor, I peered up at Ash.

"Who would do that?"

His jaw worked as he considered this. "Someone keen to keep you from discovering your magic."

A quiet breath rushed from my mouth. "The only people I can think of that fit that description are my mother and the king, and the king doesn't know I exist. Or at least, he didn't until his minions threw me in here."

I swallowed. Could my own mother have done this to me? The memories I kept buried, her screaming at me or ignoring me, all flooded my mind. I choked on my next breath. Ash touched my shoulder hesitantly, and I pressed my hand over his, relishing the warm, comforting touch.

"But she's not a mage," I whispered, unable to look up at Ash.

"Then it was someone else. It had to be a lock."

When my eyes finally met his, I couldn't stop the steady shake of my head. The only other lock I knew was Nan. But why would she want to keep me from my magic?

"Will it always look like mist?" I asked, eager to turn my thoughts to something productive and less painful than the reality that someone had *caused* me to be so bad at magic for so long—to be an outcast.

"No. It can vary, but it seems we've found your lens. You can *see* magic."

"What's your lens?"

His jaw worked a moment before he answered. "I can taste it."

My eyes flickered to his mouth—I couldn't help myself—and he noticed. The corners of his lips twitched.

"You say the mist is everywhere?"

I blinked and stepped backward, nearly toppling over the stone bench. After waving my arms about like an idiot, I answered. "Yes. Thick, swirling mist. Everywhere."

"Is there any variation in it. Say, around me?" His amused expression darkened as he waited for me to answer.

A little ashamed of how eager I was to stare at him without fear of getting caught, I took this opportunity to study him. My cheeks burned as I traced up and down his frame. "No. It's swirling around you the same as around the trees and everything else."

His mouth flickered with what might have been satisfaction, but he quickly turned away and lifted his arms. I took this moment to stare at him from this angle.

"Okay, Vera," he said over his shoulder, "you can see magic. Your own magic extends out of you, like it's something you're trying to cast off rather than harness. That might be another reason you've struggled to access it on demand. Try to reel it in, concentrate it within yourself instead of letting it leak out and…" He flinched. "Just try to contain it, okay? If you do that, you might have a better idea of what the magic looks like."

For a moment, I stared blankly at the blueish mist. I imagined myself inhaling the magic I'd let out, though I wasn't sure if this was how it was done. Until a moment ago, I'd had no idea magic leeched from me like water from a cracked vase. My eyes widened as the blue and silver mist separated, silver droplets trickling toward me as the blue mist continued to dance in the air.

Ash licked his lips and rubbed his beard with his hand. He must be able to taste the shift in the magic in the air. "Now, when I try to enter your mind, focus on the mist. Watch what it does. Follow it. Predict it."

It was difficult to watch the mist instead of him, but I did. The sparkling blue swirls didn't simply curl into little whirlpools, but they stood upright and zigzagged and splintered like lightning bolts. There was nothing predictable about the way it moved.

I stared at each little eddy of movement, but I soon became dizzy flicking my eyes toward every notable change in the mist.

"Try to see it as a whole," Ash said. He'd turned back around and was watching me.

My eyesight fuzzed a little. I tried to look for patterns, anything at all that might stand out. Within seconds, I'd found it. My attention flitted right, then left, then right, then left. I even swayed on my feet to the rhythm. It wasn't so much a pattern in the movement of the mist, which was how I'd missed it before, but a pattern in what part of it moved most notably.

A smile formed on my lips as the pattern struck me. I counted in my head, *one, two, one, two*. Then I pointed with my finger.

"There. Then there." I pointed back and forth several times, each time predicting where the next strange whorl of movement would be. "There!"

Triumph rang through my tone.

But Ash's expression stole my feeling of victory. His brow had pinched, and his mouth had hardened into a scowl.

"What?" I asked, confused at his disapproving look. "I think I figured it out. It's pointing to you. I just never noticed it before."

His face dropped. "This is when I normally leave. As soon as someone starts to uncover who I am, I slip away."

My heart stuttered. "Leave?" I stepped forward. "Leave with me. Ash, I can unlock spells. I can get us out."

A heaviness weighed on his expression when he looked up at me. "The Labyrinth has no exits, Vera. Key or not, there's no escaping. I made sure of that."

He stalked off toward the crumbling abbey. I hobbled after him, my feet still sore despite the new boots. In my mind, I saw the padlocked door once again, tempted to shove all my pain away again. I longed to put aside my discomfort once more, but Ash had warned me not to.

"Ash! Wait. You're not leaving, are you?"

He hesitated before a vine-curtained doorway. "There's something you should know, but I locked these memories within my own mind a long time ago, so no one could ever pull them from me or alter them. I can't tell you unless you break that spell, and you've got to get a lot better at magic before I willingly let you start unlocking things inside my own mind."

Desperation flowed out of me, but I didn't care. I'd never *been* a mage until this moment—all the other small flashes of my magic had been chance, unpredictable and unrepeatable. But all this time, I'd had magic right at my fingertips. I was exhausted and exhilarated, and I couldn't bear the thought that I'd already disappointed someone with my new skill.

I ignored thoughts of the door that could lock away my pain and fear and stomped after Ash. Inside the ruined abbey, there was nothing but creeping dead vines, a cracked altar, and swirling blue mist.

Ash was gone.

13

A small puff of shock escaped my lips, pulling with it every scrap of confidence I'd felt a moment ago. I was now empty—squeezed like a lemon. All my exhaustion and fear rushed back now that I was alone again.

"Ash?"

Faint lines in the swirling mist curled from the doorway to the center of the skeletal abbey, as if tracing the steps Ash had taken. He'd *just* been here. Other than that one aberration in the mist, the faintly sparkling water droplets hovered like sediment in a cup, moving as if being gently swirled by an unseen hand. Dizziness washed down my spine, and I forced myself not to panic.

A chill crept up my arms. My senses leaped into full alert, searching the shadows for men-stealing monsters. This place was a trap, designed to drive me mad.

The Labyrinth tests us.

It *wanted* to drive me beyond reason, to place me in a state so unrecoverable that I forgot my own name. The mages who had built this place, imbuing it with this incisive magic, were truly dreadful souls.

"You took him," I said aloud, filling the too-quiet space with my voice. Talking to the Labyrinth didn't feel strange, the way talking to my house would. In fact, talking to the Labyrinth as if it could hear me flooded my mind with an unexpected sense of superiority.

Mad people talk to walls, my reason told me.

"I'm not *going* mad," I countered, though no one had actually spoken. "I *am* mad. I'm angry. You think you will break me." For some reason, I knew the Labyrinth could hear me. If it had a sentience, a way of knowing my thoughts, I could decrease my fear of it by talking to it like it was no more than a tangible enemy—not some magical mentality that had swallowed me whole.

The mist danced and wobbled, unconcerned with my declarations. The pattern of its ramblings became apparent the longer I stood there. Nothing about this place was accidental. Every step of it was blanketed with magic.

"You think taking him will keep me from learning how to fight back."

This thought buoyed me, and my shoulders lifted. Of course, this was why Ash had vanished. He couldn't have just *died* in a breath as quiet as the wind. He'd go down blazing, arrows flying or blade thrashing.

I paused, cutting short a long exhale. I didn't know anything about his family or what had caused him to start a war with the king or how he'd managed to live eighty long years as a prisoner in the maze he'd built, but I knew he wouldn't die without a fight, and that felt like far more intimate knowledge.

My parents' faces flashed through my mind as the name Vera Rivers ran in my head. My last name, who my parents were, everything I'd believed about myself—none of that mattered in here. What mattered here was survival. Ash had helped me survive. And he knew I was a mage—not a quarter mage with spotty magic, but a powerful mind mage capable of slaying beasts.

In the span of a few short days, this place had upended the definition of Vera Rivers.

My brow knotted, and I glared at the finger-like mist and the leafless vines on the burned stone walls. I sensed the cadence shifting in the dance of the whirling mist before I heard the sound of wingbeats.

My hands went up a split second before a crow dove for my hair. Its tiny talons nicked my upraised arm. A thousand more poured down from the trees above, their black wings blotting out the afternoon sky.

Shrieking, I dropped into a crouched sprint, using my arms to defend my neck and head, and bolted for the exit. But the door wasn't where I'd left it. I spun around, swatting and shouting at the birds—so many birds!—and searched desperately for a way out. Drops of blood streaked my forearms.

Through the encircling tangle of angry crows, the cracked altar drew my eye. It was the only thing in the ruined abbey not covered in vines. Beneath the crack in the altar was an open grate.

I yelped and darted forward, waving my hands like twin whips. How had I missed this before? My heart thumped madly in my chest. Ash hadn't vanished, he'd gone down through the grate.

Spinning, I dropped to my knees. A crow's body hit the side of my face and another slammed into my back. I hurried down the ladder into the dark.

Not a single crow crossed the threshold to the darkness below.

The chill that hugged my ankles and aching feet crept quickly up to my thundering heart and flushed face. By the time my eyes adjusted, I was shivering and gripping my outer arms with clammy hands.

Soft, damp dirt squished beneath my boots. Sticky thin spiderwebs clung to my arms, and as I stepped forward, one traced across my mouth. I swatted in a violent little circle, more scared of the unseen spiders lurking somewhere in the dark than I'd been of a murder of crows.

But if Ash had come down here, the spiderwebs would already be broken.

"Ash?"

My voice croaked, hoarse from screaming at the birds, but the sound traveled in front of me, indicating a tunnel.

I couldn't see any fog in the tunnel, although it fell in heavy sheets from the opening above, coating me in a fine layer of moisture. How odd that the mist wasn't real, yet it dampened my skin. I touched my forearm and examined the cuts from the crows' claws. My finger traced a line in the water clinging to the hairs on my arm. And it wasn't even *real*. Briefly, I shuddered to think that maybe I really was going mad. But Ash had said mind mages sensed magic in various ways. Maybe I could see *and* feel it. The air smelled damp as well, and it had since the moment I'd entered this awful place. Did that mean I could see, feel, and smell magic?

"Ash?" I called again, a little louder.

In the black tunnel ahead, only darkness waited. The darkness breathed out a frozen wind touched with the faint stench of rot.

I turned to grip the ladder once more, suddenly worried I'd made a terrible mistake.

The grate above me clanged back into place with a vibrating finality that rattled my bones. I hurled myself up the ladder, but as I'd feared, the grate wouldn't budge.

The Labyrinth had trapped me down here.

With trembling hands, I lowered myself back down into the soft mud. *The Labyrinth tests us.* The words echoed in my mind like the wingbeats of the crows above. This test would be the one to break me, if the convulsions of my terrified heart were any indication. My breaths quickened until they were sharp and loud and beyond my control.

"No!" I panted.

I couldn't give in so easily.

My lungs didn't agree. They kept sucking air faster and faster.

I searched my mind for the locked door where I could hide my fears. The terror rising inside me made it harder to find, but soon I was mentally staring at a freestanding door braced with iron. The door to the Labyrinth was not unlike this one, albeit less imposing.

Ash had warned me not to use it until I was trained, but I didn't have time for that. I was drowning in panic. The only weapon I had was this place in my mind where I could shut out unwanted thoughts.

The door waited, ready to swallow away whatever I desired. The darkness, the crows, the *being alone*, the unknown, the aching fear that I'd never see Ash or my brothers again. I stuffed every bit of what frightened me behind that door and slammed it shut.

My knees buckled. I swayed against the ladder, barely grabbing it in time to keep from falling into the mud.

When I straightened up, I was breathing evenly.

Birds scattered somewhere above me, and my eyes adjusted fully to the darkness. Curving tunnel walls stood out on either side, and a damp path reflected just enough light for me to see the short distance until it turned right.

Merrily, and slightly aware of how foolish it was to toss *all* my fear away, I started forward, cold but not yet miserable. My feet ached, and I wished I'd tossed that pain inside the locked room as well. But if madness was the monster I had to defeat in this place, pain was the crutch I might have to bear.

Spiderwebs licked my skin. I pushed them lazily away, surprised by how little I cared about them now. I let out a small giggle, triumphant that my little door scheme had worked.

Something on the ground skittered deeper into the darkness, but I paid it no heed. The absence of fear left me strangely lightheaded, like too much had been taken out of my mind at once. The tunnel turned, and though I had no light, I knew I must move forward. So I walked, using my hands as guides along the tunnel walls.

After what might have been ten minutes or an hour, I finally spotted a light up ahead, around a distant corner. As I walked closer, however, the light never intensified. I turned, then turned again, always tracing the walls with my fingers, unconcerned about the myriad spiderwebs I raked through, and still the light remained dim.

I called Ash's name again, just in case. He didn't answer.

"You left me right when I needed you," I said, finding comfort in hearing my voice over the sticky sounds of boots against mud-covered stone. "You were supposed to teach me how to do this."

No one responded. The silent tunnels yawned with a frigid breeze. My toes were going numb, like a part of me was already dying.

"Not fair," I protested, again talking to the maze. "I learn that I can see magic, and then you shut me in a place without light."

You came down here willingly.

I leaped sideways, afraid I'd nearly run into someone in the dark, and bumped my shoulder against the tunnel wall. Shock was a form of fear, but it appeared to still be possible under my current altered mental state.

The voice had sounded distant, and yet, it had felt like my own breath, both familiar and strange. I couldn't tell if I'd actually *heard* it or just thought those words. Surely, I'd thought them. But in a deep, male voice?

Despite my confusion, my heart rate remained slow and my breaths even.

I'd resorted to talking to the Labyrinth. Perhaps it was simply talking back to me. I shook my head, angry at myself for my irrational thoughts.

Madness. This place would drag it out of me. Or perhaps it would drag me out of myself. I clenched my jaw and marched forward. There would be an exit to these tunnels. There had to be. If this was a test, I was going to pass.

14

When my fingers would no longer curl into fists and my feet felt like logs attached to the bottom of my legs, I stopped. My back barely registered the chill of the wall as I leaned against it. Cold had seeped too deep into my blood.

Being this cold was dangerous, not to mention painfully uncomfortable, but my brain wasn't concerned. Tears leaked from the corners of my eyes. Normally, in a pitch black, frozen tunnel with no way out, my body would respond with heightened senses, a fluttering pulse, and that innate desire to survive that accompanied bone-deep fear.

Instead, my body was at ease, sinking deeper into hypothermia and slack-jawed nonchalance.

"I need my fear back."

Whether my voice was in my head or out loud, I didn't know or care. I had thought the Labyrinth fed on fear, that it would stop punishing me if my fears disappeared. But I was wrong. No exits had appeared, no saviors had arrived. I searched frantically for a way to unlock the door in my mind that caged my fears.

The door was still there, but it was padlocked and arrogant. My own magic had bested me, the novice, and was gloating about it. The tunnel was so dark that the images I saw in my head appeared in front of my open eyes. The free-standing door where I'd locked away my fears sat at the end of the passage, mocking me as if it were real. I was in a reality apart from that door, and yet I had to reach it, had to open it.

I ran forward on clumsy, cold feet. My muscles jerked and my limbs clunked like I was made of wood. The door remained fixed, and as I neared it, a blaze of hope sprang up, that it might in fact be real.

"Let me out," I muttered, over and over.

Let it out.

Was that me or the maze?

I stumbled into the door. My hands pressed against the rough wood and iron braces. The door felt real. Could this be madness?

My desire to escape didn't stem from fear of remaining in this dark and cold place, but from a longing for victory over this test and the need to see my brothers' faces again, when I finally left the Labyrinth. As my hands roved over the lock, I sensed it wanted something from me—a key. I had no physical key, of course, but if this door was in my mind, I must somehow have a way to open it.

But in the few days I'd been practicing magic, I'd never learned any of this.

Maybe this time, I'd shut too much of myself in the locked room. What if everything around me was merely in my head?

What if all of this was a lie?

The Labyrinth always lies.

The walls swayed, and I didn't know I was falling until my shoulder bumped painfully into the bottom of the door. My forehead hit next. My arm was so frozen I could barely feel it squished beneath me. Still, no fear laced my veins at this dreadful knowledge.

In the place of fear, anger swelled. Anger that I was losing. Anger that I might have what it took to survive, if I knew how to harness my magic—and what to do with it.

"I don't know what you want! I can't do this!"

Carefully, clumsily, I pushed myself up and traced the edges of the door with deadened fingers. They did little to help other than prove that the door stood apart from the walls, attached to nothing and with nothing behind it.

The mind mage who'd thrown me into the Labyrinth talked about how I'd been able to fight back, to resist her—at least a little. If only I'd had a tutor! If only I hadn't been shoved aside my entire life. I briefly wondered who had locked me away from my own magic for so long and why. I'd like to punch that person about now.

I would die here, in this tunnel, because I was foolish enough to attempt magic I didn't understand.

The king's bearded face swam before me, as if on the face of a playing card, the same smug, stern frown present in all his portraits. Mind magic was dangerous...outlawed...forbidden.

My stomach churned with the notion that the king was at least partially right—my magic was dangerous, and I might have just sealed my fate by using it on myself.

A new sound, small and rhythmic, jolted me from my macabre thoughts.

Footsteps.

Elation fluttered through my veins. Help was coming!

"Over here!" I shouted. Reason, fighting hard to be wise in the absence of my fear, drove a warning through me that whatever approached might not be pleasant. But reason without fear was merely blind optimism.

There wasn't one set of footsteps, but two. Possibly more. They drew nearer.

A pale light flashed at the far end of the tunnel, illuminating a small frame. Ferrier bolted toward me, her arms pumping, a strange ghostly light shining all around her. Her red hair whipped back and forth behind her head. Perhaps this place wasn't only in my mind.

I glanced behind her for Edith, but the young girl's face told me it wasn't her sister chasing her.

The locked door behind me clunked a little as I backed into it. Ferrier would slam into me in a few moments, and whatever pursued her would overtake us both. The door rattled from the other side, my fear trying to break free.

"Vera!" shrieked Ferrier, tossing a glance over her shoulder. "They're coming!"

My face fell. I had little to offer as yet more anger poured down my spine. At least the fury was warming me—but not nearly enough. I still shook from the cold.

"What is that?" Ferrier asked, pointing at the door.

So it was real to her too.

Or the Labyrinth was lying to us both.

"I, er, shut my fear behind a door in my head, and now that door just sort of showed up to block the way."

She slowed her sprint by slamming her palms into the very real, very sturdy door.

"This door is in your head? Then why am I seeing it and feeling it?" She pounded on it, as if my fear might open the door and welcome us both. Then she turned curious eyes on me. "Make it go away!"

"I...can't."

Ferrier's odd grayish light, dim but brilliant in comparison to the pitch darkness, lit the heavy wooden door and cast a melancholy hue over the cobwebbed walls and mud-dampened tunnel floor.

"They'll be here any moment," she shouted. "Vera, you've got to remove this door!"

"What's coming?" My voice was measured and unconcerned, clearly frightening Ferrier even more.

Footsteps, in the tell-tale thump-thump-thump-thump of cantering hooves, rounded the corner at the far end of the tunnel.

"The wraiths."

I swallowed. Reason had little to offer this pronouncement, other than the utterly unhelpful advice to promptly find a way out.

I shoved my hands helplessly against the door. "I'm so sorry. I can't open it. I don't know enough magic!"

Ferrier stomped her booted foot and jabbed her finger at the door. "Yes, you do. I've never seen anyone manifest from their thoughts like this."

In history class, we'd learned that mind mages of old, before and during the war, could make things appear—manifest things—simply by thinking them into existence. It was what nearly caused the king's troops to lose, battling an army that could bend reality to their whims.

Ferrier whimpered. The charging sounds thundered closer.

"If you really did make this door, that is," she grumbled.

There it was, the doubt. Maybe this door had been here all along, another test of the Labyrinth, not a manifestation of my thoughts.

Dark shapes draped in fluttering cloaks now clogged the tunnel where Ferrier had first appeared. They cowered against the ceiling, bent low over the necks of near-skeletal horses.

I should have feared the galloping wraiths. The locked door. My imminent death. But instead, I imagined that the door was simply on the other side of us, between me and the monsters.

Ferrier yelped and I inhaled in shock as the door blinked from one side to the other. Two breaths later, the wraiths slammed against the door.

The freestanding door in the center of the dark tunnel hadn't left enough room for a human to squeeze past it, but the bone-thin arms of the wraiths reached around the wood with ease, and my jaw clenched at the notion that these creatures might have no trouble slipping past the door. But silver mist, illuminated by Ferrier's magical light, rushed from around us and pushed violently against the fluttering cloaks of the wraiths, preventing them from reaching us.

Ferrier's screams turned manic. She began to shake, her arms jerking as her eyes widened and she stared at the rattling door. She couldn't see the mist holding them back.

Slavering sounds and hard *thunks* filled the small space as the wraiths—whatever they were—fought to shatter the barrier between us.

Even though I was now on the opposite side of the door—the door I'd assumed was the one holding my fears—no fear returned to my mind. I merely stared at the door, then at Ferrier. I sensed that everything was wrong, but there was a dullness in my limbs and in my mind as I tried to process our situation.

"We should go."

That was the logical response.

It was odd not to be afraid of the sounds, so otherworldly, that curled around the edges of the door. Dark fingers tipped with fragmented black claws, reached through the mist toward us on either side of the frameless door. Ferrier's breaths turned to ragged, lurching things.

She was losing herself to her fears.

"They can't get around the door," I told her. That might be a lie, but she needed a reason to look at me, to listen to me rather than their noxious snarling.

With a shaking, frozen hand, I led Ferrier down the tunnel, uncertain whether I'd sealed our pursuers off or sealed us *in*. As we walked, Ferrier's screams became loud wheezes, then breathless notes of despair.

"Ferrier," I said, using her name as a way to anchor her.

She didn't look at me. Her arm was mostly limp, and her expression vacant. She still had a magical glow around her, but it was dimming, and the tunnel was growing darker once again. Madness was slipping in, and I had no idea how to stop it.

"Look at me, Ferrier. We're going to get out. Those things back there can't get to us. We're going to be okay."

My words flitted over her like a breeze, barely stirring her from the throes of her fears. Walking beside someone so afraid, when my own fears were entirely gone, evoked a strange sensation inside me. I wanted to wrap her in a blanket, tuck her into a warm bed, and sit beside her, telling her stories until she fell asleep. But not here. Not now. We had to keep walking.

The tunnel narrowed as we walked. My reasoning brain wondered if we were moving deeper into this trap.

That wouldn't do.

We stopped to rest, and I never took my cold hand out of Ferrier's. She needed to know she wasn't alone, and my fingers were so cold that the hand not linked with Ferrier's lost feeling quickly. I leaned against the tunnel wall, hating the way its cold stole more of my own heat, but relishing the small relief from the long walk. Ferrier tipped against me, and I wrapped my arms around her shaking body.

She sobbed quietly into my chest.

If Edith were here, she'd know what to say to her sister to quiet her fears. I rested my chin on top of the girl's head and pinched my eyes shut.

Tiny shards of warmth prickled through me, and a quiet sob of joy slipped from my trembling lips. My shivering had turned to violent shuddering, but as we stood there, my chest stilled to an intermittent trembling. Another moment to warm up, then we would proceed.

As we waited, I envisioned exits in every possible way.

Nothing had changed. The darkness around us seemed to grow deeper as Ferrier's magical light continued to dim. Her crying had stopped, but her eyes still stared absently into the darkness. She was slipping away, and I had to do something about it.

"Tell me about your magic," I said, trying to hold her back from the edge where madness lurked.

She shivered and said nothing.

I was out of time. If we didn't get out of this black tunnel, I would lose her. Edith would lose her. My mind flashed to Archer and Danny, and I pushed away from the wall, guiding Ferrier at my side. If I was faced with losing either of my brothers to the fate of mindless wandering, I would tear the world apart to prevent it.

A wave of sadness struck me, and I steadied myself against the cold tunnel wall. It felt different. I'd only taken two steps, but the wall here wasn't stone. It was earth.

My fingernails curled into the dirt. It was entirely too soft for comfort, like a mere touch could bring the walls crumbling down. I swallowed. If my mind had been able to fear, I would have frozen in terror. A stone tunnel might not collapse, but one carved out of dirt certainly could.

I squeezed Ferrier's hand and closed my eyes.

In my mind, I made a last attempt to get us out. Every other kind of door I'd tried to conjure with my mind hadn't worked. Trap doors, side doors, even windows in the ceiling. The Labyrinth wanted something else from me. It could no longer drive me to madness through fear, so it wanted to drive me to madness another way. This test was for me, but it was also Ferrier's test.

How she'd been separated from her sister, I didn't know, but the Labyrinth had placed someone deathly afraid in the company of someone incapable of fear. Suddenly, I knew what the Labyrinth wanted.

The way out was simple, as if the Labyrinth had written it plainly for me. The magic all around me, though I couldn't see it in the darkness, swarmed in my mind. As Edith had mentioned, I *could* feel it. My own magic had connected with the magic of the tunnels, and I searched out the space, realizing exactly what I needed to do.

But I couldn't do it. The way out would push Ferrier into the abyss.

My eyes popped open. Ferrier's magical light had vanished. She still clung to my hand, shivering in the dark. Her breathing had intensified again. Doing this, even if it meant freeing us, would crack what little remained of her sanity.

"Unfair," I murmured into the dark, hating this place for what it was asking of me.

Ferrier didn't respond.

There had to be another way. My mind could almost taste the fresh air on the outside of this forsaken tunnel. Maybe it was in my head, but I sensed the cool mist writhing on the other side of these earthen walls. Freedom was so close, yet to break us out would be to drive Ferrier into madness.

I didn't think it would work, but I tried explaining it to her.

"I think I can get us out."

No response.

"I can feel the outside. It's so close, Ferrier. I can get us out. I just have to break through."

Her breaths were featherlight and fast. Still no response, but her fingers clutched mine tighter.

"You need to trust me."

I felt her hand tugging against mine even though I couldn't see her. She was shaking her head, violently.

"Edith said not to trust anyone who said that!"

Her hand yanked from mine before I could tighten my grip. She took off farther down the pitch-black tunnel, running so quietly I feared she'd vanished. I tore after her, but my movements were slow from the cold.

Soon, I heard another sound over my footsteps and breathing.

Cantering.

The tunnel wraiths had returned.

Dirt began to rain down over my head. Twice, I heard Ferrier whimper, but I couldn't catch her. Blast my frozen feet! I tried to call out to her magic, tried to find her mind with my own and slow her steps, but I had no idea how to do magic like that. If only I could keep her sane while I broke us out of here.

But I hadn't learned enough magic yet. I could feel the Labyrinth's magic all around me, now that my mind had latched onto it, but I couldn't feel Ferrier's mind. The magic of the Labyrinth felt like an ocean of cold, a sea of infinite glass shards crashing endlessly into my consciousness, uncomfortable but mesmerizing. I ran slower than normal not only because of my tired, cold state, but because my mind was so consumed by the discovery of this magic.

Ferrier's muted footsteps and fearful breaths drifted further ahead.

"Ferrier, stop!"

The sound of the wraiths was coming from up ahead. There must be a web of connected passages down here.

When the cantering stopped and a sickening snarl paired with a high-pitched scream, I knew I had no other choice.

I pulled the entire tunnel down on top of us.

15

Dirt rained down on my head. Its weight crushed me. I fell with a thump as air was pushed from my lungs. My limbs tangled, and my frozen skin burned from unexpected heat.

Absence of fear is a strange thing when one is dying. I lay there until the dirt settled, and the only noise I heard was the faint rustling of the breeze through the trees.

I was out of the tunnels.

I lifted my head, dirt running in rivers off my head and down my neck. It was day.

"Ferrier," I coughed, spitting out clumps of moist earth. I heaved myself up and climbed atop the mound of earth. Blue mist swirled in hurricanes, while shards of silver fog pulsed from my body into the air, mingling once again with the Labyrinth's magic. Stone walls rose on either side, and skinny trees grew in the narrow path, reaching up to the sun high above. My hair fell into my eyes, along with tiny specks of dirt. I coughed and rubbed the dirt out of my eyes.

The space between the walls was wide compared to the tunnels, and my eyes burned as they adjusted to the light of day.

"Ferrier!"

I glanced around, and even as I looked, the dirt from the tunnels sank into the earth. Soon all the ground around me was flat.

"Ferrier!" I screamed again. I began to run, but at the first step, shards of pain in my calves brought me back to the ground. Tiny knives stabbed my frozen muscles. I stayed on my hands and knees for a few moments, breathing heavily.

"Ferrier?" I called, my voice weaker. I crawled forward.

Had she even been real? Had she truly been with me?

My reason began to crack, the fracture splintering outward, growing larger and larger.

"Ferrier. Ferrier. Ferrier." I muttered her name over and over and tucked my chest against my knees, pressing my forehead to the ground.

It couldn't all be fake. Some of this had to be real. The pain I was feeling was real. My feet—they were throbbing. They were cold. I was so cold.

I shook. As I shook, more dirt tumbled off me, out of my hair and off my back. Footsteps neared and I looked up. A lone figure approached from between the ever-changing walls. It wasn't Ferrier. It was a man.

At first, it looked like the man wore next to no clothing, but as he neared, I realized his clothes were simply so dirty, it was hard to determine what he had on. He was barefoot. And his knee was bleeding.

He walked with a vacant expression, his mouth slightly ajar and his muscles slack. He didn't look at me as he passed by. I shuddered and scurried away, placing my back against the stone wall, but I quickly jerked forward just in case the wall decided it wanted to crumble on top of me because I had touched it.

The door that caged my fears shook and rattled against my consciousness. If it burst open now, I might drown. Go mad in a single breath. I couldn't let that door open now. Not when I knew how much fear I'd bottled up behind it. The man, who must have been one of the Nameless, ambled absently, a slight limp to his gait.

I coughed up a piece of dirt that was lodged in my throat. He turned at the sound, his eyes searching vaguely until they landed on me. Then he hunched his shoulders and walked toward me.

"I can't help you. I'm sorry. I need to find Ferrier."

I scrambled to my feet, choking out gasps of pain as I stumbled away. Reason was enough to tell me to distance myself from this Nameless man, so I ran along the wall.

The Labyrinth—or whoever was controlling it—stole more of my reason with each step I took. The walls wavered. I was pretty sure I saw a tree take a step.

Ignore it, I told myself.

For all I knew, not a single thing I saw was real. The magical mist that filled this place seemed to be having a riotously good time, sensing my demise. It whirled and waved in its own merry little circus as my mind began to snap.

The Labyrinth felt its victory nearing.

I reached a right angle in the wall and turned. Through the trees, pale gray stone walls came into view. My hands slammed into the rock. I was trapped. It was a dead end.

I spun around and stared at the man still stumbling toward me. He made strange, unintelligible sounds—groanings and mumblings—that grated on my remaining sanity.

"Edith!" I shouted. "Ferrier! Ash!"

The Nameless man only seemed to sense where I was when I shouted, so I clamped my mouth shut and, with a deep breath, lunged into a sprint back through the forested Labyrinth, past the Nameless man, the mist stinging my face as I ran.

"Edith!" I called. "Ferrier!"

Up ahead I saw red hair. With a surge of relief, I recognized Ferrier's short frame. She was stumbling along much like the man who was by now far behind me. Dread pooled in the pit of my stomach as I neared her.

"Ferrier?"

She didn't turn toward me. I ran around her and looked her dead in the face.

"Ferrier?"

Her brown eyes slid vacantly toward me.

"No!"

But it wasn't my voice that uttered the sentiment I felt.

"Ferrier!" Edith screamed and ran from a small opening between the walls to my left that had been concealed by vines. She raced forward and wrapped her arms around her sister, then began to shake her.

"No, no, no. Ferrier, listen to me. Ferrier!"

Ferrier's head lolled, and her neck slumped backward as her sister tried to shake her back to her right mind. Edith reached a hand around her sister's neck and supported her head, then tucked it against her shoulder and wept softly. After a heartbeat, her eyes slid over to me. In them was a murderous darkness.

"What happened?" she snapped.

I swallowed, cringing as more grit slid down my throat.

"We ran. I was in the tunnels. There were wraiths." Guilt forced my words out in a fitful confession.

Tears spilled down Edith's cheeks as she held her sister. A scratch on Edith's right cheek bled, and her knuckles were bruised.

I took a deep breath and started again. "Ferrier found me in the tunnels. There were wraiths chasing us."

Edith coughed. "You saw the wraiths?"

My eyes pressed shut at the memory of the horrid creatures.

Edith stared at her sister. "They got to Ferrier."

I offered a small nod. "The only way I could get us free was to break out of the tunnels. I knew it would frighten her—she was so scared already—but it was that or..." I didn't finish the sentence.

When Edith's eyes met mine again, anger rolled off her like steam from a boiling pot. Her face was flushed, but it deepened to a shade almost crimson. Her cheeks trembled as she released Ferrier and stepped around her.

"You did this."

Those three words were the single worst statement I'd ever heard.

She launched herself at me, going straight for my throat. Before I could say anything, she'd slammed me to the ground. I felt like I had in the stream, as the kelpie almost drowned me, except this time I wasn't afraid. Exhaustion and shock slowed my limbs, and I barely fought back.

"What's wrong with you? Aren't you afraid to die?" Edith shouted, releasing my neck. In a single movement, she rolled off and scooted backward, grabbing her sister's hand, as if appalled by her own actions.

I stood, one hand on my neck. "I shut my fear away."

Edith scoffed. "The Labyrinth will kill you now," she said over her shoulder as she gathered Ferrier into her arms, leading her forward. Ferrier mumbled something, and Edith pressed a knuckle to her mouth, then shook her head. "If it can't drive you mad, it will send all it has after you. I don't want to be here for that."

I couldn't blame her, and I didn't want to put her and her sister in danger, so I watched her go. The crack in my reason splintered a little more. Alone had never felt like such an empty word as it did at this moment. Even the walls seemed to loom closer above my head. And then I realized that's exactly what they were doing—they were closing in over me.

With a desperate inhale, I scanned the mist, looking for anything that might give me an edge over this miserable place. If the magic had a tell, I would find it. I would *not* allow this place to bury me in its rubble. A brief memory of the crows flooded my numbed mind, and I frowned, recalling that the Labyrinth didn't like to be *one-upped*. Edith was right, it would throw everything it had at me now. The magic of this maze was concocting some trial that would fracture the remaining bits of my sanity like a stained-glass window at the mercy of a hammer.

I jammed the heels of my hands over my eyes and tried to think. Whatever the next trial was, it wouldn't aim at my fear or my pain, as I could lock those things away. The Labyrinth would send something to attack my reason, my lone remaining survival instinct.

The approach of feet drew my eyes away from the patterns in the dizzying mist. I looked up. Edith was running back toward me, ushering Ferrier along quickly beside her. Ferrier ran clumsily, her arms straight at her sides. As they ran past me, Edith looked up at me with narrow, angry eyes.

"Back that way, there's a—" But before I could warn her of the dead end and the Nameless man, I saw what had chased them back this way.

Loping wolf-like creatures with limbs as long and skinny as table legs bounded toward me. Their claws tore up the earth, and their backs were so ridged along their spines they looked like they could be part dragon.

Skinny tails with tufts of fur at the end whipped out behind them. I counted six before I turned and ran. I passed Edith and Ferrier within a few steps, which didn't seem fair. I stopped and turned. I wouldn't let them get eaten by these creatures, not when it was my fault they were coming.

The door in my mind rattled, but I ignored it. I stepped in front of Ferrier and Edith, planting my legs wide. The six slobbering wolves raced toward me. I drew the knife at my hip and held it in one steady hand, then I searched for the magic of these creatures, as I'd done with the minotaur.

Without fear, I could fight these beasts until my dying breath, which would give Ferrier and Edith time to get away. I would not go down without at least trying to help them.

Now I wish I'd kept the bow. Ash's bow could have taken out one or two of these beasts before they got to me. But it was just me and the dagger.

And my mind.

I would need to be able to tolerate pain to win this. Recalling Ash's warning, I pictured a second door in my mind, building in a tiny window this time, and prepared to shut my pain away as the first two dogs sailed past me on either side, arcing wide.

No!

I hurled my dagger at the wolf on my right. It sank into the animal's ribcage, and a loud yelp rang out. With my body angled from throwing the blade, I didn't have time to turn before the next wolf was upon me. Its snout slammed into my leg, biting down hard.

For a split second, pain blinded me. But in a heartbeat, I slammed the door over my pain, and only a small pinprick of discomfort remained.

It had worked. The small window in the door had let a little pain seep through, but not enough to overpower me.

Struggling to shake the wolf off my leg, I spotted Edith and Ferrier up ahead. Edith stood in front of Ferrier, whose back was against the wall. She too held a small blade in her hand as the uninjured dog ran straight for them.

I pictured a cage around them, protecting them. I should have put the cage around the dog instead—should have learned more magic!—because as soon as the bars appeared around my friends, the creature leaped up the iron bars, teeth bared as it dropped down onto Edith's shoulders.

I curled into myself as the wolf standing over me placed a paw on my shoulder and crushed me to the ground. Its bite stung, but less than it should have.

I kicked at its underbelly, my foot connecting with soft flesh. It huffed and backed off, giving me a moment to flash another thought toward Edith and Ferrier. I pictured them on the other side of the massive stone walls, something the dogs couldn't scale, and then the wolf was upon me again.

I rolled to avoid its next bite. Its snout snapped at empty air, but two other wolves quickly joined the attack.

The animals converged on me. I hoped my magic had worked and Edith and Ferrier were safe, but I couldn't hone in on their magic when my mind was preoccupied with the wolves. I envisioned a dagger, quickly realizing, with a stab of foolishness, that I should have imagined something that would incapacitate all the animals at once. But I had no more time. Fangs snapped at me from all around.

I jabbed the knife and missed. Teeth broke into my skin and blood poured out, but I barely noticed.

Reason gave way to whatever madness lay beneath it and I screamed.

Maybe it was anger or maybe I'd finally let go of my reason, but I lifted my arms, slashed them outward, and shouted, "Enough!"

At once, all six monsters were thrown back as silvery mist blasted away from me in a circular wave. The wolves crumbled to the ground, dissolving into the earth the same way the minotaur had, leaving nothing behind but tiny wisps of ash.

Ash.

A brief thought tortured my mind as I imagined the boy I'd kissed floating away in the breeze like those miserable creatures.

Chest heaving, I stood, frozen to the spot with my arms outstretched. The mist jittered and buzzed, as if frantic, even angry, at my victory. It rushed back toward me, washing my skin in an unsettling chill.

Footsteps crunching leaves.

A shadowy figure.

I wasn't ready for another monster.

My mind reeled. My eyes flickered madly at the swirling mist, hunting for a pattern, a warning that might show me where the threat was. It licked and danced and seemed to point toward the approaching figure.

Then I heard a familiar voice.

"Vera." My hands dropped to my sides as Ash stepped into view, the mist a silent vortex around him.

16

The wall behind me trembled, causing the ground to shake. The sounds of stones grinding and scraping against each other obscured all other sounds. I couldn't tear my eyes from Ash or miss the way the mist licked at his sides and his hair, as if warning me about *him*.

"Vera?" Edith called after the walls stopped changing.

The trees stilled. At once, the silvery-blue mist whirling in the air paused, as if the entire Labyrinth were holding its breath. Ash eyed me up and down, then darted past me toward Ferrier and Edith. I whirled around and followed him.

Ash paused before reaching them, his hands tense at his sides.

Edith was standing over Ferrier's body, breathing in ragged gulps. Ferrier twitched in little movements, but her eyes remained vacant.

"No. No." Edith lifted a hand as Ash took a step toward her. "Don't come near her."

"She's not too far gone. I can heal her," Ash replied, to my surprise.

Edith's mouth parted, and her trembling stopped. Before she could respond, he had stepped forward and was kneeling in the leaves.

Chewing my lower lip, I watched him. The pattern in the mist was undeniable now. It blinked around Ash like a thousand tiny candles, dancing and cavorting in little eddies that all pointed to him.

Ferrier moaned and rolled to her side. Edith dropped to her knees beside her sister.

"What happened?" Ferrier muttered, her eyes no longer vacant but sharp and alert.

Tears poured down Edith's face as her shoulders shook with quiet sobs. Her eyes lifted again to Ash, flicked briefly to me, and then moved back to her sister, who she dove to embrace. Ash stood and faced me.

And all the mist—every sparkling droplet of it—moved as he moved. Then it began to converge on him, slowly at first, every droplet condensing and moving from the farthest reaches in the trees until they lit upon him like an army of infinite fireflies.

His jaw worked, and I remembered he said he could taste the magic. He inhaled and every ounce of the blue mist disappeared into his body. My mouth hung ajar. Edith must have sensed something, for when I glanced back at her, her eyes were fixed on Ash. Ferrier, too, stared up at him from the ground.

"It's you," Edith said, helping her sister to her feet.

Ash turned so that he could see me and the two sisters. He nodded slowly.

"That's why the Labyrinth always responded to you. Because..." Her voice trailed off.

"He's the one who built it," I said, my words smaller and quieter than I'd intended.

Ferrier squeaked and scrambled to her feet, tugging her sister farther from Ash.

"I'm also the reason you found what you needed," he added, his tone a little sharp.

Edith wrapped an arm around Ferrier. "The Labyrinth only gives us what we need right before sending us another test. *You're* the one who told us to never trust the Labyrinth. Never trust what helped us yesterday."

Ash turned toward me, ignoring Edith. "Vera, you need to let your fears back out. The Labyrinth is angry, and it will not stop punishing you for shutting your fears away." He hurried to my side. "I never meant to leave you, but when I stepped into that abbey, the door spat me out a long way away."

I nodded and pushed open the door in my mind. My heart beat quickly, and panic spidered outward from my chest to my fingertips. My fears had returned.

Ash grabbed my shoulders. "Good. But you need to take control of your magic, now, Vera."

I scowled, unable to drag any words out of my tight throat. Edith pulled Ferrier's face against her chest and began backing away.

"Every time you tear apart a piece of this place, you risk all our lives," he muttered, but the others still heard him.

Ferrier tugged her sister's arm in fright as they edged away from us.

"Wait," Ash said, lifting a hand toward the sisters. They hurried away faster, and he shouted louder, pointing at Ferrier. "I healed her." But they only turned and ran. "I kept you alive," he shouted at their retreating forms.

With my fears surging through my mind once again, I grasped for something nearby to clutch. There was nothing but the stone wall a few steps away, and I stumbled toward it, bracing myself against it. As my chest tried to draw in air, my throat closed until my breaths sawed in my lungs.

He squeezed my shoulders and pulled me against his chest. "Take control, Vera. You can do it. Bring your magic back to yourself."

I took a deep breath and nodded. The silver mist around me flickered, and I feared I'd once again lose my ability to see it. As I had with the minotaur, I envisioned myself taking hold of the mist and pulling it toward me. The faintly glowing magic slowed its endless whirling and slowly converged on me.

"That's it," Ash whispered.

After another deep breath, pale water droplets beaded on my arms and hands, and the remaining silvery mist hovered calmly in the air.

Ash let go of my shoulders but didn't step away. "I want to show you why I built this place, and you won't like it. But I want you to know. And I need you to see what's happening when you tear it apart."

I briefly recalled Nan's words about Ash—that the truth was nothing like what I'd learned. If what he wanted to show me would bring me pain, I didn't want to see it, but I needed to know the truth about him.

His words about tearing apart the Labyrinth intrigued me. I lifted my hand toward his. If I could tear this place apart, then I could get back to my brothers, keep them from ever having to suffer this fate. Perhaps if he showed me how he built this place, I could find a way to tear it down and set us all free.

As my hand reached slowly for his, he said, "When I let you in, you will see a keyhole. Open it."

I put my trembling hand lightly in his, and he guided it up until he placed my fingers on his forehead. My hand jerked as I pulled away, surprised by the way my hand on his head evoked memories of the way he'd kissed me.

"I've kept this truth buried inside me for eighty years," he muttered. "It might come out a little forcefully. But I promise I won't hurt you."

I bit my lip and reached for his forehead again. He leaned forward into my palm, and a small breath breezed from my lips that moved the tiny hairs beside his face.

"I'm going to show you now."

17

Blue mist rose out of him and encircled my hand. Soon the connection was too strong for me to remove my hand, even if I'd wanted to. The glittering water droplets crept up my arm, along with a tingling cold.

In a breath, the mist both consumed me and sank into me. I was no longer standing in front of Ash against the Labyrinth walls. I was facing an elaborate keyhole suspended in space. Silver mist reached from me toward the lock and wove through the small hole, eliciting a faint *click*.

I was staring at a man wearing a golden crown in a small room with a round table and latticed windows. Two other men stood to the side of the room. My hands were chained in front of me. Cold metal pinched my wrists and ankles.

"You will do this," the king said. "This will be your prison, built by your own hands, to contain everyone like you—everyone capable of doing what you have done. Every mage who enters your Labyrinth will be one less to threaten our world, and it will be your magic that sustains it. Forever."

I glanced out the window, anger simmering in my chest. "No one lives forever," I grumbled.

"But you will."

I frowned. There was but one way a man could live past the bounds of his natural lifespan. "You claim to hate my magic, yet you bid me use it to stay alive?"

He thrust a finger at me. "You took the minds of so many, giving yourself power, sucking it from those who had no choice but to give it to you." He leaned forward, pressing his chest against the table. "You will continue to do this. Endlessly. From each mage that dies in the Labyrinth," he said, jabbing his finger into the table so hard his skin turned white, "you will siphon out a little of their life to extend your own."

My blood seethed. "When I did that before, it was to save a life."

The king scoffed.

The face of a woman flashed through my mind. I'd extended the life of the woman I loved, not knowing it would start a war, and yet, after all that happened, after all I tried, her life was only hanging by the most fragile of threads. Now that I was a prisoner, the king could will her death or her life by the flick of a finger.

"You will write this into the magic of the Labyrinth. There will be no escaping it." The king jerked his head toward the two mages standing by the wall. "What you did to us, we will do to you as you are crafting this prison. We will ensure that it is built exactly to our liking." The threat in his voice was obvious. The king and his mages were going to invade my mind and use me as a tool.

As I'd done to countless others.

My teeth ground together, but there was little I could do to resist this man. I'd lost. Despite all the power I'd accrued, I had still been overcome.

"Part of your punishment," the king said, standing, his fists braced on the table, "will be to live forever with the knowledge of what you have done. And even if you seek atonement, it will never come. You will see each mage who enters the prison weaken and die within the walls of your Labyrinth, fed the poison of their own magic. And perhaps over time, as you see each one of those mages as the enemy they truly are, you will begin to feel the weight of what you did. Of who you are. And if it begins to grow heavy on you, it will still never be enough." Spittle flew from his lips at the last word. "Now go."

He flung his arm wide and turned toward the window. Instinctively, I reached for his mind, but barbs had been placed around it by the mages standing in the room to prevent me from entering. Even under the magical cage I was in, I still had more power than they knew. But it was less, it was weakened now. They had stripped everything from me.

The king moved toward the door, and I had but one chance to say something before he vanished.

"How are you and I any different?" I asked, voice low.

The king paused at the door, and I might have imagined that his shoulders trembled. "You and I are nothing alike."

He stormed from the room, leaving me with the two mages.

The memories shifted. I was standing in a forest surrounded by people in dark cloaks. My body couldn't move. I was no longer chained in iron, but I was more confined than I'd ever been, chained by magic. The magic caging my body forced me to turn toward the man standing behind me. His small crown glittered in the moonlight. Beside him, six other mages stood, should I try anything.

"You will build the prison here," the king said. "You will make it inescapable. You will build madness into it that will drive even the strongest to their knees. You will strip the ability to think from every meddler who enters my kingdom. And as you build, remember our bargain. She will be healed, but first you must build."

All I felt was anger as my muscles moved without my consent toward a freestanding blue door waiting in the dark forest ahead. Though I hated this feeling, I walked willingly, seeing the face of a woman—the woman I loved—pale and nearly lifeless. If I completed this task to the king's liking, she would be spared. After so much death, one life was all I cared about. If she lived, I would wander this world forever, in a maze of my own making.

"You will use your magic under my command this time, and you will use it to save this country from the likes of you," the king bellowed as I strode toward the door.

And with that, a feeling like a boot in my back sent me through the door. It shut behind me. And though I knew there was nothing magical separating me from the king anymore, not until I built it, I also knew that I was forever alone.

Twenty men and women stood before me. They faced away and their hands were shackled behind them. Some were shaking, others crying. Without hesitation, I pulled their consciousnesses into my own, and they fell to the ground, lifeless. Their heartbeats would return if I finished my task quickly enough. In the last battle, I'd employed five mages to fuel my own magic. With the power of twenty mages, I could tear the foundations of the earth apart.

But despite the immense power at my disposal, the king's mages were still trapping my desires, and just as he'd planned, I began to build. I called up walls and trees and traps. Then I saw *her* face, and my concentration wavered. But the king's mages gripped my mind and shoved it away from thoughts of my love—the woman I'd started and lost a war for.

I had a task to complete, and I knew the king's mages wouldn't kill me. Death would have been too easy. The power of all the Guilds whirled in my mind and I directed them as I saw fit, pulling stones from the depths of the earth to do my bidding. Every time my magic surged toward something the king did not desire, the chains on my mind tightened, and I was forced to relent. The king's mages were always watching, making sure I did as he commanded. Of all the mages in his kingdom, I was the only one capable of building this place he so desperately desired, the only one capable of wielding so many minds at once and locking in place the magic as I went. An odd irony, given that he'd wanted to eliminate me in every battle we'd entered over the past year.

In order to drive mind mages mad, this place had to sever them from their sense of control. I wove magic into the walls, the water, the earth, the seeds I planted, the very air itself. This was magic as I'd never used it before—creation that fueled itself as I went, as if my mind, empowered by the magic of so many others, was a fire that grew stronger with each passing minute.

Soon, I lost myself to the frenzy of this creation, pouring my mind into the maze like a soldier bleeding out upon the ground.

Everything I built was both true and false. The trees were alive, but they never stayed in one place. The walls were solid, but they moved. Everything within the Labyrinth told the truth as often as it lied. Because what was more maddening than being lied to?

The pale face of the woman I'd loved floated in my mind, and the rage mounted.

I brought every dark and nasty thing within my mind to life.

Soon I was kneeling on the ground, exhausted from the effort of building. But I was not yet finished. In order to keep the magic of the prisoners from breaching the walls of the Labyrinth, I had to ensure there were no cracks, no fissures, no doors my mind might have hidden in my subconscious as I built. I planted my hands on the ground and sucked in a deep breath, diving deeper into the magic at my disposal.

If I drained the energy of the mages fueling me, as well as my own energy, I'd kill them and likely myself as well. I'd learned in battle, when the concept of stealing magic from others was still new to me, that a mage only had so much magic to give before their power—and their life—expired. I'd also learned that right before a mind gave out and its owner died, I'd sense a hole opening up in the fabric of my consciousness.

Several holes were now apparent as I reached for the magic I needed to finish this prison. I did not want to kill again, but the king's control on me was unrelenting, and he wouldn't let me stop until I was certain I'd completed the job. Gritting my teeth, I stretched out on the forest floor, ready to sink into the sleep that would come when I released the other mages' minds from my own and sealed myself within this house of madness. The Labyrinth needed to be inescapable, the king had said. But the mind was a powerful thing, even when it was consumed with so much magic, and it *wanted* a door.

So with a final surge of magic, I discovered a single door, far beneath the ground, that my mind had left for me. It was inaccessible, but it was *there.* If I used magic to destroy this door, I and all twenty mages fueling me would surely die. So, instead of making it a door that led back to the mortal world, I altered it so that it would lead me, when I was finally ready, to the wretched embrace of death.

After locking every spell in place, I let the energy of the other mages go until it was only the chains of the king's mages remaining on my mind.

I lay on the forest floor for a moment, breathing. Feeling the scattered parts of my mind coming back together with only my own consciousness within the walls of my skull. The emptiness was vast, and for a moment I was utterly confused.

"It is done," I croaked, exhaustion overtaking me.

The vast magic in this place made me taste metal and salt, as if someone had poured an entire cupful into my mouth. My tongue was so dry and my desire to drink so strong that I could barely form words.

Seeing this place, the prison my magic had built, the Labyrinth that was my soul laid bare, a dark and twisty maze with madness at its center, I saw for the first time the blackness of who I was. Every monster was a creation of my own mind. Every wicked trap a small section of my soul. The king, enemy that he was, had a reason to fear us.

With a single exhale, the chains on my mind were severed, and I was left alone within the Labyrinth.

The memories shifted violently once more, and my eyes focused on a young woman, perched in a web of poisonous vines. She wore a gray wedding dress and stared down at me with narrow, curious eyes.

Her magic pulsed from her along with the tang of mint. As soon as her magic had entered this place, I'd felt it—the tug of a loose thread that had begun the unraveling of a great tapestry. As her magic slipped from her into the air around me, my awareness of every space, every corner, every monster in this place faltered. I lifted my bow, terrified that she might be a key, an untrained one at that, and her presence here could mean my undoing.

My body lurched and my head hit something hard.

I blinked and saw a bearded face.

Ash's face.

I pushed against Ash's mental hold and fought to regain control of my mind. It was like pulling my brain out of deep, sticky mud. My forehead throbbed where I'd collided with his chin, and the small sensation anchored me to myself, to my thoughts, to my body.

Ash's fingers wrapped around my wrists. I tried to move away from him, but the information he'd shared with me weighed on me like an iron blanket.

"Stop," I snarled, curling away toward the wall. "I don't want to see anymore."

He released me and raked both hands through his hair. "Now you know the truth," he said, his voice gravelly and raw. "Each enchantment that you break here tears apart a piece of my mind. If I go mad, I can't keep anyone safe anymore, and the monsters will be free to do as they were told."

He lifted his hand but froze before touching my face. Instinctively, I whipped my head aside, afraid that if he touched me, I'd be trapped by his magic once again.

His expression sagged a little. "I wanted you to know the truth. I'm sorry if it...disturbed you." His next words came fast and low. "Filled with the power of twenty others, I could have stripped the world bare and rebuilt it as I had once planned. Yet, as I began to manifest the outer walls of the prison I was building around myself, I saw visions of the blood I'd spilled, the dead faces of those on the battlefield who'd dared come against me when I was at my strongest."

I blinked, picturing the army of skeletal shadows that I'd seen in the dogwood grove. "You showed me that nightmare already," I muttered, still shaken by the onslaught of his memories.

Ash's jaw clenched, and he shook his head. "I haven't allowed myself to think of that grim sight in years. I'd shut it away, buried deep in this place. Then you arrived, and the horrors I'd blissfully forgotten came pouring out of their confines."

"I didn't do it on purpose," I reminded him, bracing myself against the stone wall.

"Your fears were manifesting things you didn't understand. When your magic entered the Labyrinth, it connected with my own and..." He paused to run a hand over his mouth. "I had to find you, to destroy you. I couldn't bear what your magic was doing to me."

I stepped away from him, barely catching his next words over the snapping of a twig beneath my boot.

"And then I saw you."

My mouth opened, but no words came out.

"I saw you, and I couldn't do it. I tasted the wild magic all around you, and I sensed you weren't tearing me apart on purpose. I wanted to help you, like I helped the others, in the hope you would learn to control your magic."

A gentle breeze lifted the hair beside Ash's face. The blueish mist that pulsed around him floated toward me once again. I tucked my hands behind my back, but I couldn't deny that my heart tumbled sideways at his words. His magic hovered before my face, mingling with the silver mist spilling from my own skin.

At the gentle touch of his magic to mine, I let out a bottled breath. It felt warm this time rather than cold, and the light sparkled like the facets of a diamond in sunlight.

The king had built the Labyrinth; Ash had only been a tool. He'd crafted all the monsters, but only according to the king's desires. All in an effort to save one woman.

I stared at the leaves over my head, where glittering blue and silver mist rioted in the sunlight. It reminded me of the peculiar way snow in winter caused the air to glow when billowing down from tree branches. It was beautiful—dangerous and lovely, a mad mix. All of this magic was his. Everything here. Every monster was a part of him.

"Who was she?" I croaked, thinking of the woman I'd seen in his memories, the one he'd admitted he started a war for.

Ash dipped his chin. With eyes downcast, he said, "She was the king's sister. I'd fallen in love with her, despite my lack of royal blood. She'd loved me, too, or so I'd thought. She wanted to run away to be with me, considering she was already betrothed to another man she hated. I promised her I could make it happen. Arrogant fool that I was, I planned to use magic to alter the memories of her guards and anyone who witnessed our escape. I failed. We were caught. But I didn't give up. I promised her I would grow powerful enough to create the world she wanted."

He flashed his eyes at me, then looked quickly away before continuing. "She told me I had to become powerful enough that the king would never think of breaking us apart. While I worked furiously to gain power, the king got wind of my growing abilities, and he sent his spies to eliminate me. That only made me fight harder. Despite what the king thought, I never wanted the throne, I only wanted him to approve my betrothal to his sister, which he would never do unless I bested him. Then she got sick, and I didn't see her for a month. I stole magic in that time, and when I learned she'd grown sick to the point of death, I blazed into the palace and poured my magic into her, trying to save her." Ash's throat bobbed twice. "It didn't. It pushed her into the place between living and dying that suspends life. And then the man she'd been betrothed to, the one I thought she hated, stormed in and declared I'd killed his wife. In that month when I thought she'd been ill, she'd gotten married instead. It was all a lie. Her illness was feigned, and I nearly killed her."

As he spoke, I'd stopped moving. I pinched my lips between my teeth and stared at Ash, trying to ignore the aching sensation in my chest. His eyes remained fixed on something to my left.

"She said she loved me," he scoffed. "But when I proved too weak, she married another man. It drove me to madness. I wanted to consume more power than ever. I wanted to destroy the world she'd chosen, but I also wanted to heal her. So she could see that I'd become what she'd always wanted." His knuckles cracked at his sides. "But I failed."

My throat was dry, but I croaked out the words, "Was she ever healed?"

Ash hung his head and kicked a mushroom poking up through the leaves. "The king said he would heal her if I surrendered and built him this Labyrinth. I was shut in here before I ever learned if he'd kept his word."

Pain lanced through my ribs. "The king's sister, you said? Her name was—"

"Evelyn," he finished.

My eyes closed slowly as I nodded. "She died of old age when I was young."

Ash lifted a hand and raked it down his face. His mouth opened, then snapped shut. "She lived."

I offered another small nod. Nan was right about one thing: his wounds were deep. So deep, he'd locked them away with magic and destroyed the key. It was not unlike the way I shoved my darkest thoughts away behind closed doors. I'd inadvertently dug up everything he'd tried to hide—no wonder he'd been so hostile at first.

"Without you," he said, "I never would have thought of Evelyn again. I never would have let myself face what really happened all those years ago. So, thank you."

He stared at me with raw desperation, waiting for me to respond. Sometimes truth can hurt more than a lie, but I was glad he'd told me all of this. Now I knew the truth about Henry

Asher, villain of our era. And I had an idea—a wild one, but one I couldn't stop thinking about.

I reached for his hand, pulling it up so I could link my fingers with his. "Thank you for showing me. Now, I think I know a way to get us out of here."

18

Ash's eyes brightened as I took his hand, but at my words, he shuttered his expression once again. "Vera, I've told you. There's no way out."

Trying not to let his words discourage me, I lifted my shoulders and stepped around him, staring out at the forest. "No, listen, you made this place to *lie*. You said it yourself. It lies about everything, including the fact that there's no way out."

"That's impossible."

"No, it isn't," I said confidently. I was fairly certain that I'd figured out something he'd been too blind to see. "I'm going to find Edith, Nan, and Ferrier, and we're going to go home."

"Vera, wait." He reached for my arm. The warmth of his fingers on my skin sent an extra wave of heat up my already flushed skin. "This place is not going to just let you leave. I built it so that..." His voice was strained, as if his words were coming out through a sieve. "I built it so that no one could get out."

"No, you built it so that no one would *think* they could get out."

His eyes narrowed. "My magic didn't leave a loophole that big."

"Oh, but it did," I said, unable to hide an eager smile. "One you didn't even see. Come on, I'll explain as we go."

His brows lowered briefly, then his eyes bored into me with renewed vigor, like he could see what I'd seen in his mind—the secret he hadn't known was there. A secret he'd locked away.

"You mean the door," he muttered.

I grabbed his hand, and his eyes widened at my deliberate touch. "Yes, the one you buried!"

His eyes pinched at the corners. All around us the mist zigzagged in angry little fits.

Linking my fingers with his, I muttered quietly, "I'll show you."

This time, his eyes closed slowly, his hand tightening around mine. Then his jaw fixed with a tight frown.

"I saw it when you built this place," I admitted. "But I don't know how to get there. You'll need to show us the way."

For eighty years he'd been lying to himself. There *was* a way out of this place—I'd seen it in his memories. There was a bit of madness in him, after all, the kind of madness that could turn a lie into the truth.

He fixed me with a serious expression that bordered between hurt and hungry. I studied his face, trying to memorize every plane of it. Then, his mouth softened and he brought my hand to his face. His lips brushed my palm, and I gasped.

"You deserve to have a life, to find happiness." His words whispered against the soft skin on the inside of my wrist. "If there were a way out, I'd take you there. But there's not." He lowered my hand. "Stay here with me. I will do my best to keep you safe."

For a second, it was hard to breathe.

My mind flooded with memories. Sitting in the schoolhouse, listening to our instructor rattle off war stories his father had told him. Phrases like *the villain of our age* and *a man with a heart of pure evil* were a sharp contrast to the image before me. A man broken from his choices, literally trapped in guilt and anguish and heartbreak. Stories of what he'd done to increase his power by stealing it from others had laid the foundation for my fear of mind magic.

He was the reason I had feared the magic in my veins, and yet he was also the reason I'd finally found it. I shook my head. No, it was stories of him that had founded my hatred of mind magic. This man, the one standing in front of me, had saved my life, taught me how to access my magic, and shown me I wasn't a piece of straw to be tossed out or burned.

He was the reason I no longer feared mind magic.

"Come with me," I begged. "We can all get out of here. I can show you what you never allowed yourself to believe."

He watched me with piercing eyes, trying to read my thoughts as my expression shifted.

"Isn't it funny," I added, "that the king, in his effort to eliminate us all, threw me in here, the key that would unlock the Labyrinth?"

His thumb brushed my lips, and I breathed in against his calloused touch. He bent his head toward me so I was temporarily blind to everything else. "Ironic, indeed." He kissed the skin beside my ear, his beard scratching slightly as he moved to kiss the other side of my face. "Okay, little key, I'll take you to the door."

We walked quietly back toward the fort, picking our way over brambles and around trees. Somehow, the silence we shared felt more intimate than all the words we could have said. I trailed my fingers through the blue mist, its cool sting reminding me of the memories he'd shared with me. It was strange to recall someone else's memories as if they were my own, but the longer I pondered them, the less tangible they became.

The tall trees, the vine-covered walls, the eerie narrow paths to my left and right, all of this—all the monsters and the madness—was the result of a broken heart.

My magic's silver mist alternated huddling in droplets on my arms and leaping into the air to turn little circles around me. If it weren't for Ash, I'd never have realized the truth about my magic. I'd never have *survived* here long enough to know I was a mind mage, and a powerful one at that. I had lived within a prison of sorts for years, thinking I had no place in this world but one of rejection and failed magic. He'd been the one to tear that prison down.

Anger bubbled up inside me at the way the king's sister had treated Ash. She'd had a man's entire heart—something I'd only dreamed of—and she'd thrown it away as if it meant nothing to be loved.

But that didn't excuse what he'd done. It didn't erase the atrocities he'd committed in his attempts to gain power. Nan's words echoed among Ash's memories. *Try to forgive him.*

The Labyrinth seemed particularly agitated today, as walls kept popping up, funneling us through a part of the forest with a larger concentration of evergreens. Despite the ever-changing path, Ash directed us with ease. All around us, his blue magic sparked in the air.

As one wall leaped up to block our path, I whispered to Ash, "Let me try something."

I approached the stone wall and ran my hand over it, picturing a door like the one I'd seen in that wall by the creek days ago.

Behind the netted ivy, a door materialized.

Ash coughed and stepped up beside my shoulder. "How did you do that? These walls are impassable."

I shrugged. "That first wall I saw, the one that knocked you out, it had a door in it too."

He turned skeptical eyes on me. "That's how you were able to steal my bow."

I jabbed my elbow into him. "Come on."

⊱⊰

When we stood beneath the fort once again, I hesitated, burdened with the idea circulating in my head. If I was wrong...we could die. I shook away the notion. I wasn't ready to accept life in this forsaken place. I *had* to try.

Ash waited below as I shimmied up the rope, faster this time but no less awkwardly.

"Nan," I said, hurrying to her side.

She looked up from her book, her white hair catching the sunlight. "What's the matter, my dear?"

"We have to leave. Ash told me I can break this place apart with my magic. I think I can get us out."

Nan's hands pressed down into her lap. "There is something I need to tell you as well, dearest. I wanted to wait until I knew your magic was strong and fully free."

"Free?"

Ash had said someone had locked my ability to see my magic.

Nan held my gaze as she said, "Years ago, right after your first sign of manifesting magic, I made a choice. Even though it wasn't law yet for every mind mage to be thrown into the Labyrinth, I saw a pattern in the king's increasingly intolerant attitude toward our magic. He wanted to eliminate us, and I couldn't let that happen to you. I wasn't certain if you'd manifest, and if you did, what kind of magic you would possess, but there were times I thought I felt your magic, and it *felt* like mind magic, which has innumerable nuances but always feels cold to me. Fire magic, of course, feels hot. I knew that if you turned out to be a mind mage, that you'd likely be thrown into this prison. So, without even telling your mother, I placed a binding enchantment on you that blinded you to your own magic."

My stomach lurched, as if I'd fallen off the edge of the platform.

Nan closed her eyes briefly. "I'm sorry, child. I believed it would keep you away from this place. I didn't want you to be without your magic, but I was so afraid for you. I wanted you to live freely." Her face fell. "I was wrong. You were brought here despite my best efforts to protect you."

"Protect me?" My voice cracked at the word. All the condescending comments, disgusted looks, and disappointed moments of my life bubbled up in my memories. "You stifled me. Made me an outcast."

My heart roiled like bubbling wax. I loved my Nan, and yet, learning what she had done left me with a hole inside that drained away all feeling until I was a hollow shell.

Tears leaked down her cheeks. "It was out of an effort to save you. I see now it was futile. And no words can express how much it pains me to know that what I did was still not enough to keep you out of this place. Can you forgive me, my child?"

At her tears, my anger cracked and my hollow shell quickly flooded once again with care for the woman I'd always admired, always loved. I dove for her, swallowing her frail body in a careful hug.

I would never be the same because of what she did to me. But just knowing that she loved me, that her choices were intended to protect me—it was all I needed. Love came without borders, and if forgiving her was what I needed to bridge the chasm that had just opened up between us, then I would do it. I'd already lost her once, and I didn't want to go through that again.

Her muffled words hummed in my ear. "I love you. I'm sorry I made your life more difficult."

I pulled away from her, tears warming my own cheeks now. "I can see my magic now. It looks like silver mist."

The corners of her mouth pressed into a proud smile. "I bet it's beautiful, just like you."

I laughed and wiped my tears away. "Come on, Nan, let's get out of here."

Her smile faded. "I'm not going anywhere, dear."

"What?" My chest tightened.

"I'm too old to get myself down from this loft. I'm too old to traipse through a prison full of monsters."

The pronouncement weighed on me heavier than the darkness in the tunnels.

"But I have to get out. To save Danny and Archer from whatever the king tries to do to them. I can't let them...I won't..."

"There, there. I know well the feeling of wanting to protect those I love at any cost."

My throat burned as I tried to swallow. "If I can unlock part of this place, I can't let you stay!"

She took my hand in hers. "Vera, I've made up my mind."

I backed up as a wave of sadness threatened to crash over me. I didn't want to lose Nan again. Holding on to a branch, I leaned out over the edge of the fort and called for Ash. In a moment, he climbed into view and joined us on the platform.

I planted my hands on my hips. "Can you convince Nan that she's coming with us?"

Ash peeked around me at Nan. "No. She's as unyielding as her magic." He nodded at her with a faint smile touching the corners of his lips.

Whirling on Nan, I huffed, trying to think of what to say to change her mind. Before I could craft my argument, however, Ash cleared his throat, drawing my attention back to him. His face was down as he spoke, his expression concealed by his hair falling over his shoulders.

"Even if you're right about the door, I can't come with you," he said. "I can never reenter the mortal world. I must live in this limbo forever, between life and death, paying for what I did. I'm sorry, Vera. Besides, if I ever leave, every monster in this place would be able to leave too. There would be no one to keep them from escaping through an unlocked door." Breathless, he said again, "I can't come with you."

19

My lips parted and the breath sucked from my lungs. A door in the floor of my consciousness opened, and I fell through, sinking into a vastness that I hadn't known existed within me. I had been alone before. I had felt empty before. But there had always been Archer and Danny. My mother's rejection had hurt continuously for years. And now I realized that I had used this space to shut away feelings of emptiness and loneliness as well as hurt. In my weakest moments, I'd had this trapdoor, and I'd shoved my feelings down into it and locked it, over and over again. And now I'd fallen into them. I was drowning.

I pressed the back of my hand to my mouth and pushed past Ash, dropping to the lower level of the platform. For several seconds, I stared at the massive tree trunk, shoulders heaving up and down as I tried to make sense of Ash's words.

When I felt him approach behind me, I spun and glared up at him. "You think you're too wicked to be happy," I snapped.

A hardness crept into his features.

"You believed what the king said, didn't you? That you can never atone for your actions."

His jaw flexed.

"Just because we all have the potential for evil doesn't mean we're all as evil as we can be. It's our hearts that make the decisions. If we built a Labyrinth to mirror our souls, each one of us would have dangerous beasts inside. Yes, you chose wickedness for a time. But you've changed. You even said yourself you've tried to keep everyone alive here."

Nan hummed her agreement from behind him. I'd nearly forgotten she was listening.

"But people have died here. And many others have gone mad," Ash countered.

Nan's voice cut through our little argument. "The king forced you to do this, to lock that magic in place. It's not your fault the people here have gone mad—it's the king's."

His eyes flicked toward her. "I did it willingly," he muttered, as if afraid to voice the words. "I thought I was doing the world a favor."

"No!" I grabbed his hand. "You must stop punishing yourself. Besides, you can restore their minds. You can set them free, like you did for Ferrier."

The skin around his eyes loosened as sadness washed over his features. "I don't think that's possible."

I wasn't deterred. Shaking his hand up and down as I spoke, I pressed him to understand. "They're mind mages. Your Labyrinth has control of their mind. If this Labyrinth is *you*, then you have their sanity somewhere tucked away in one of these corners that keeps shifting. The Labyrinth feeds on fear and breeds madness, but *you* have control over the Labyrinth."

His eyes narrowed, then widened. My words pricked something deep within him—guilt...and perhaps, a flicker of hope.

I smiled at him. "We're going to get out of here, and you're going to restore the minds of all these people."

He shook his head. It was a faint movement, barely noticeable but for the way his hair twitched at the sides of his face. "I can't do that."

For a moment, I studied his face, searching for answers hidden beneath the surface. He had an entire history I didn't know, a past more haunted than I could imagine, and he was capable of terrible things. I should want to walk away from him, to nod politely and let him let me go. Instead, my blood heated at the sight of him, and I felt pulled toward him as if we were magnets drawn toward each other across space and time.

"Nobody should have the potential to do what I did."

I recognized in him the same veiled sadness I'd carried for so long. Mine had hardened into anger that only required the tiniest prick to rise up into rage. The anger pinching his brow had the sting of guilt, and his guilt had been powerful enough to manifest a prison for himself.

"I used to think of myself as *less than* everyone else who could do magic at will," I said, crossing my arms over my chest as memories nipped like violent little monsters in my mind. "I hated that everyone overlooked me, that my magic was broken, so I shoved all my hurt and anger into a part of my mind I thought I could ignore. But pushing my problems away never solved anything. You can't bury your guilt here and assume it'll stop bothering you." I loosened my arms and placed one hand on his chest. My skin tingled as the rhythm of his pulse echoed up my arm. "You tried that. It hasn't worked. You need to leave it behind."

When movement caught my eye, I jumped a little. Nan had risen to her feet and was grasping a branch for support. Her eyes were red with tears.

"Nan. Come with us!"

"No, my sweet girl."

I rushed to her side.

"I am sorry for the way you felt. It's my fault." She patted my arm. "You and the others must go and find this door you speak of. I will stay here and search out every monster I can find. I may not be able to dispel them like you, my dear, but I will tie them to this place so that they can never leave, even if there is a door. I will buttress this place with all the magic I possess, so that Ash can leave without it crumbling down and loosing all these monsters into the world."

Ash's warm hand latched in mine, and I squeezed hard, a rush of tears warming my eyes.

"And you'll need someone to lock the door behind you when you go," she added with a small smile. "So that no one else will have to face the madness here."

"Nan, you can't!"

She waved me off. "I can and I will. It will take some time, but I will do it."

Ash stepped around me and placed his other hand on Nan's shoulder. "You'll need someone to show you where all the monsters lurk. I will stay with you until it's finished." She patted his knuckles, then leaned her cheek against their overlapping hands.

Meanwhile, my heart imploded at the thought of leaving them both in this wretched place. I stepped toward them.

"My sweet Vera," Nan said. "I'm sorry I caused you so much pain. Let me do this for you now."

"Nan, I can't lose you again."

Her soft, cool fingers cupped my cheek. "You can't keep me, either. Time will make sure of that." She reached up to pat Ash's face next. "But you can keep him. And together, you can find the happiness that was stolen from you both."

Walking away from the fort tore a little part of my heart in two. Nan's embrace lingered on my skin, and the warmth of her hands covering mine rattled my thoughts as we searched for Edith and Ferrier.

Goodbye would never feel sufficient. But there was no changing her mind. Ash's presence ahead of me as we walked comforted me. He would take care of Nan until the end, of that I was certain. She would be the poles holding this place up so he could leave. Without her, he could never walk away from the Labyrinth.

"They're just ahead," Ash said, turning to face me. He took my hands in his and tipped his forehead against mine. Silver and blue mist entwined all around us.

Ash looked at me the way I'd dreamed of being looked at my entire life. I closed my eyes as I tried to burn this memory into my mind. A tear pressed down my cheek.

"Vera," Edith's voice pulled me out of Ash's grip. I peered around him, the ghost of his touch still warm on my face.

I ran toward Edith. Ferrier walked out of the misty forest behind her sister.

"I can get us out of here," I announced.

Edith's eyes went wide.

"He explained it all. I understand it now."

"But there's no way out." She glanced behind me at Ash, and a look of mistrust darkened her features. "Why is he here?"

"I saw everything. He's not who you think."

"Maybe he just made you believe that. Everything here is a lie, you know. You can't trust him."

Doubt slid a cold finger up my spine, but I shook away the feeling. "I saw inside his mind. What could be more real than that?"

Still her eyes squinted when she looked at Ash. "A way out, you say?" For several heartbeats, I thought she might say no. Then she pressed her hands to her face, and sobs burst from her mouth.

"There is a door," I said, turning back to face Ash. "I saw it in his memories. He can take us there." I hesitated before adding,

"He built it as a door to death, but he built everything here to lie. The door doesn't lead to death."

Ash's face went pale.

Edith emerged from behind her hands and gaped at me. Ferrier stepped up and looped her arm through her sister's.

"What do you mean?" Ferrier asked.

Ash rubbed his beard. "She thinks the door will lead back to the outside world."

Ferrier smiled. "The Labyrinth always lies, right? I like Vera's idea."

Bless her. I returned her smile.

Edith shrugged. "All right then. I'm willing to look at it. But no promises that I'll go through."

"That's fair." I looked up at Ash. "You'll need to show us the way."

He worried his lip with his teeth. "I don't know the way. I locked a spell in place to ensure I didn't go searching for it."

"Then let me in again," I whispered. "I'll find it."

The blue mist of his magic stilled from its frenzied dance and slowly converged on us. Edith startled, sensing a change in the magic around us, though she couldn't see it.

The blue mist settled on my skin like a million frozen snowflakes, then sank into me. For a moment, my skin looked foreign in an icy sheen. Then I was in his mind again. I was still aware of myself this time. Briefly, it felt like true madness, seeing myself from his eyes and seeing him from my own, two consciousnesses mixing as one. But my brain quickly adjusted to this duality of input, and it felt like being in a dream, where I could see myself and be myself simultaneously.

I took in the Labyrinth from the mind of its maker.

His fingers, still linked with mine, tightened until my knuckles cracked, as if he were afraid of what I would find buried in the depths of his mind.

I could find any answers I wanted. Answers about *her*.

It was tempting to dart like a thief through his memories, learning everything I didn't know about him, answering every question I could think of. But if I was right about the door—about him—I'd have time for that later. So I inhaled and began searching.

The entire Labyrinth was spread before me in Ash's consciousness. It was much bigger than I imagined, and there were so many people in it. I could feel them all, their minds brushing against my own. Part of my own.

His own. I was in Ash's mind. I had to remember this or I would lose myself.

I could feel all the walls. I could sense all the monsters, moving, chasing, hungry. But I knew what I was looking for—the place that would contain the door I needed, the door that I alone could open. It would be the very center of this place, the darkest part of Ash, the part that he had buried the deepest.

Because when he was building this place, he'd built it to lie. He built it to lie to all the people who would ever enter it, but he also built it to lie to himself—to cover up what he had done, and to distract him from the pain that had led him here. He might have denied it for a long time, but he still carried that heartache within him every moment of every day. I squeezed his hand.

I took a deep breath and then surged forward, pulling him along with me. Part of me was conscious of the world around me, of Edith and Ferrier following behind. I could feel their minds...and their fear.

There was so much fear here, so much madness. It swirled and lurked. It writhed like snakes. There were so many Nameless and only a small handful of mages who had not yet succumbed to the madness. Some of them were far away, while others were quite close. But I charged onward, taking first a right turn and then another. The walls shifted and moved, opening for me as they had for Ash. Would he allow me to get to the darkest part of him?

My worries were shared with him, and his mind answered me.

Even my darkest secrets are yours, his voice intoned inside my head. *I won't hide myself from you, but you won't like what you find. It's a door to death, not life.*

I still believed I was right. *The Labyrinth lies. You built it that way,* I reminded him.

He tugged briefly on my hand, and I spun to stare up into his face as we walked through a narrow, curving section of walls. *It's not a lie you want to test.*

Aloud, I answered, "How do you know?"

Edith glanced between us, a confused look on her face, but she said nothing.

Silently, inside my mind, Ash answered, *It's not a lie I want you to test.*

My heart pinched painfully in my chest. I offered him a half-smile and pressed onward. *Let me at least show it to you. I think you'll see I'm right.*

Until he stopped me, I would keep going. And Ash could stop us anytime he chose. He could set every monster in this place upon us or bind us with vines, as his magic had done once before.

We clambered down a stairwell that looked like ancient stone steps, yet I knew they were only eighty years old. There was nothing truly ancient here, though perhaps the depth of the ache inside of Ash had crafted a world that was already broken when it first came into being. Perhaps there had never been anything but ruins here.

Down. I knew we had to go down. A stone amphitheater opened up before us. This must be part of it, for it descended down to a cracked stage surrounded by crumbling stone benches. I hurried down, no longer holding his hand. I could feel the minds of Edith, Ferrier, and all the others in this place. It was strange to be one with the Labyrinth, the way he had been for so many years. To sense the minds of so many at once and to feel their fears.

It stabbed at my own heart. It threatened to close my throat. Breathing was difficult with the weight of so much fear and madness weighing on my mind.

When we reached the amphitheater's floor, I glanced around. We had to go deeper. I whirled around and caught sight of Ferrier still descending the stone steps of the amphitheater.

"Ferrier, we're going to have to go back underground. Can you do that?"

Her face paled, and her head began to shake.

"I promise we will be okay. The wraiths won't get you. I won't let them. He won't let them." I placed a hand on Ash's shoulder. "All of this is his. And it won't hurt you now."

But Ash turned toward me, and I felt his mind within my own, shifting. The amphitheater morphed, its stones cracking and splitting. Dirt tumbled down as a tunnel opened up beneath the steps.

"That's it!" I rushed toward it.

"Wait," Ash said. Suddenly the magic was yanked out of my mind. I gasped and stumbled forward. I fell into the stone steps beside the entrance to the tunnel and turned. Ash stood over me, his magic no longer linked with mine.

"If we go in there, every monster in this place will come after us. I cannot keep you safe in there."

"Yes, you can." I stood up, my chest close to his.

"No. This place will descend on us. It doesn't want me to leave. I'm tied to this place. If it senses that I'm attempting an escape, it will throw everything it can at me—at anyone who tries to leave. That's what this place does, it kills those who try to leave, as the king commanded."

Ferrier clapped a hand over her mouth. Edith wrapped an arm around her sister's shoulder.

"You crafted this door to be your final escape," I reminded him. "It's a way out, I know it."

"If death is your way out, then, yes."

"I still think you're wrong." I glanced at them, arms wide. "We have to try."

Edith shrugged. "I at least want to see the door. Come on, Ferrier. You can do it. I won't let anything happen to you."

"Ash, I know you'll keep us safe. You won't let them hurt—"

"It's not like that. Of course, I want you to stay safe. I've tried to keep everyone in here safe and alive for years now. But I've failed. I created this place with the magic of twenty mages. I can't defend against everything that's in here. Not when it's all coming toward us at once. And it will. It's coming now."

The blue mist twirled in agitated spirals. This place *was* angry at us.

"Then we should hurry," I said and darted into the dark tunnel.

20

My footsteps echoed down the long stone corridor and back again.

I pictured a light hovering before me, and to my delight, a glowing orb bobbed along the top of the tunnel ahead of me as I ran. It was so much easier now that I could see and manipulate my magic, but with each spell, I felt a small tug on my bones and muscles, the price of the magic. My legs ached a little now, and I was reminded of Ash mentioning how tired he was after creating the Labyrinth. Or the times I'd seen Guild members stumbling along the roads toward their luxury club, where they'd sleep off the exhaustion brought on by doing magic.

This magic was really so simple, I had no idea why it had taken me so long to learn it. It seemed more like faith than magic—all I had to do was trust that it would work. I wondered if doubt, even more than skill, was what separated the weaker mages from those with greater power.

As we pushed deeper into the tunnels, an eerie chill swept over me. The mist pricked my skin, as if fighting my presence here. It stung and grew so thick that it was hard to breathe.

We'd reached the heart of the Labyrinth.

We stood at a convergence of four tunnels: one turned to the right, one to the left, and one continued straight ahead. I stopped and spun. Edith and Ferrier caught up a few steps later, our loud breaths the only sound for several moments.

"What now?" Edith asked.

I glanced at Ash. He appeared uncomfortable, as if his very soul was exposed. We had come to the darkest part of his heart, the center of the maze, but also the exit. I sensed that he had always tried to avoid this place. In the eighty years that he'd lived here and walked this maze, he had never once come here.

Cantering hooves echoed down the corridor. I glanced to my left.

"They're coming," Ash said.

Ferrier whimpered and grabbed ahold of Edith's dress. "The wraiths," she whispered.

"They won't get to us." I closed my eyes. I knew I didn't have long. None of us had long.

I looped my hand under Ash's arm and muttered against his ear, "Let me in, one more time."

He did. It was only a second, a pair of heartbeats, and yet it was so full of pain that I recoiled. But I found what I'd hoped to find: a locked chain surrounding a blurry, dark shape. In Ash's mind, I tore off the chains.

This time when I opened my eyes, a similar door to the one I'd seen at the entrance of the Labyrinth stood in the center of the crossway, only it was covered in cobwebs and black with mold.

Edith screamed and jumped backward. "Where'd that come from?"

Ferrier lifted a finger and pointed at me. "She can conjure doors. She can manifest. I've never met anybody who could do that!"

"It was already here," I said with a shrug, not sure what to do with the compliment.

Ash stared at the door. In the pale, bobbing light above our heads, his face took on a ghostly appearance, but I sensed it had more to do with the turmoil inside. Blue mist swarmed around him like a horde of angry bees, but around the door, the mist fled, leaving a space vacant of Ash's magical haze. I stepped into this space and reached for the door.

"Vera, no. That's the door to death. I know it. That's where I placed it. I placed it right here. I remember now."

"No, listen," I said. The cantering sounds of the wraiths' skeletal horses grew louder. I couldn't tell which tunnel they were coming from or if they were coming from all four directions. The ground beneath us began to tremble, bits of dirt and rock fell from the tunnel ceiling and clattered onto the stone floor. Ferrier pinched her lips.

Ash muttered a few words, and a blue-tinted barrier burst across each tunnel, silencing the sounds of the approaching wraiths.

Edith's eyes grew wide. "The only way out is to go through that door?"

"Will we die if we do?" Ferrier squeaked, her confidence from earlier gone.

"No. No, we won't. That's what the maze wants us to think." I stared at Ash as I spoke. He needed to hear this more than the rest of us. "Ash, when you built this place, you believed that you deserved to die, that this place itself was a mercy of sorts. But the truth is that none of us can pay for what we've done. I used to think that I was good, and that I didn't deserve to be in here. But if all of us have to pay for what we've done, not one of us would ever pay enough. Nan's actions, my mother's, my own—none of us could claim that we were free from guilt. We have to go through that door. We have to be willing to accept that the only thing we have to pay with is our lives. This door summed up what you felt when you made it, that death is the only way out, and yet, you told me you made everything here to both lie and tell the truth. It's an *exit*, Ash. It is the way out, just not in the way you thought."

He lifted a hand and wrapped it around the back of my neck, pulling me toward him. His warmth pushed away the cold air of the tunnels and all the fear that had built up inside me. Here, I was safe. Even in the darkest part of this Labyrinth, with monsters bearing down on us, I'd never felt more alive. I'd finally found someone whose arms felt like home. Whatever was coming down those tunnels, I didn't fear them as much as

I feared losing him. Learning to survive the Labyrinth with Ash had forged a bond stronger than anything else I'd ever known.

Before he pulled away, his arms tensed. A wave of apprehension flooded my senses.

"I will find you when this is over," he said, pressing a kiss to my temple. "Now unlock it."

I spun toward the door and let my magic slip into the keyhole. I found the spell and, as I had with the monsters, I dismantled it. A feeling like being thrown from a horse pushed me into Ash, and at the same moment, his protective spell around us dissolved.

The tunnels began to shake. The walls were crumbling around us. This time, I knew that if they fell, I would not be climbing out of the rubble.

The thundering hooves of the wraiths drew closer, faster than my beating heart. Chunks of dirt and rock collapsed, covering the tunnel floor and knocking against my shoulders and my upraised hands.

This place wanted to bury us.

The snouts of the wraiths' horses burst into view, converging from all four tunnels. Beneath the echoes of the hooves came deep, ragged snarls. More than just wraiths headed our way. Silver-blue mist clashed against itself in the pale light around us. I lunged toward the door.

"I'll go first," I shouted.

But before I could take another step, the ground beneath me shook so hard I fell. Warm air seeped from beneath the door, caressing my knuckles.

A single breath escaped my lips as I scrambled for the door handle once more, but a creature launched itself from the darkness of the tunnel and crashed into Ash.

The wraith had the long limbs and upright body of a human, but its skin was a dusty gray. Its hands were tipped with cloudy black claws.

A silent scream clogged my throat even as my fingers closed over the knob. If we could walk through the door, all of this would end. I shoved my shoulder against the door, and it swung open, bleeding a bright light into the collapsing tunnel. When I cringed away from the sudden brightness, something grabbed my ankles and pulled hard. I yelped and lost my breath as my chest hit the ground. Despite digging my nails into the tunnel floor, I was pulled away from the door, away from my freedom.

Edith and Ferrier both screamed, but I couldn't see them.

With a sudden pulse of magic, Ash sent three of the creatures flying backward. They thudded against the walls and slid to the ground. Ash kicked the wraith holding my ankles and sent it tumbling down one of the tunnels.

As I rolled to look at Ash, a strange ink-like shadow leaked from the crumbling walls, filling the poorly lit tunnel with thick darkness. Ash dove on top of me, covering me. His hands cupped my head and tucked it against his throat, but before I lost sight of the tunnel, I smiled as Ferrier leaped through the open door.

We rolled until I was up against the wall, Ash's body protecting mine from the monsters that were now swarming the tunnels. I heard a scream, and I tried to look up, but Ash's grip was tight. I hoped Edith had made it through the door.

"Let me go. I'll go through."

"They won't let you!" he shouted between clenched teeth.

I peeked an eye open to see Edith fighting two wraiths.

"We have to help her!" I shouted into his ear.

"I can't let you go."

His words filled the part of me I'd kept locked away, the emptiness where I'd shoved all my hurt and anger and sadness over the years. I wanted to kiss him, but considering the circumstances, that didn't feel right, and my cheek was still pressed against his hair.

I turned my head and stared at Edith, who'd also fallen to the tunnel floor. With one quick glance we made eye contact. In that breath, I pushed all my magic toward the wraiths clawing at her. Two of them reeled backward as if slapped, silently dissolving into the darkness, and Edith stabbed her dagger into the one directly over her. Its dripping black cloak melted onto the tunnel floor as the creature vanished. Edith glanced my way once more as the next monster leaped toward her. I felt like a horse had trampled my whole body, but I pushed a little more magic out. Silver-tinted mist swarmed around the wraith's face, stalling it for a moment. Edith hopped up, grabbed the door handle, and dove into the light.

I shoved one hand onto Ash's shoulder and pushed myself up. He sat up with me, pulling me into his lap as a wraith sliced a hand through the air right where my head would have been if I hadn't moved.

I pictured an invisible barrier around us, but my mind was frayed at the edges, and the barrier wouldn't last more than a few seconds. "They went through! Let me go now."

Ash's gaze lit my skin on fire, nearly causing me to forget the monsters all around. His blue magic braced my flimsy shield, and he pulled me against his chest.

The silver-blue mist didn't budge as the monsters clawed against it, unable to pierce the now solid dome created by our mingled magic. For the moment, they were unable to reach us. Together, we could pass through the door unscathed and enter the world beyond.

Outside our little bubble, the tunnels crashed in on themselves. A massive rock *thunked* to the ground between us and the door.

My heart somersaulted. If I didn't move right now, I could miss my chance and get buried down here where Ash kept his deepest secrets.

"Come with me!" I gasped, hammering a fist into his chest.

"No. You were right. I need to set the rest free."

I stroked his fallen hair out of his face and kept my hand on his scratchy beard.

He tipped his forehead against mine. "You set me free, Vera Rivers. Now go, find your happily ever after."

My throat clamped shut, and my tongue stuck to my mouth. A small croak was all that came out when I tried to respond. So I pressed my lips to his instead.

He was warmth and fire and home.

And for a single breath, he was mine.

Then, something large hit the door, knocking it shut and hurling us into pitch darkness once again.

Ash hopped up, bringing me to my feet with him. "Go," he said, and kissed me once more, hard and desperate.

"I'll wait for you, as long as it takes."

Ash had to give this place up. But in order to do so, he had to admit that there was nothing he could do to pay for what he'd done. I couldn't do that for him. He could never atone for what he'd done, and only when he was willing to admit that, to give up trying to outweigh his bad deeds with the good and die to his former self, could he come through and find life on the other side.

I knew it with such certainty that I wondered how he could be so blind as to miss it.

"I will come for you," he said.

A broken, gasping laugh fell from my lips. He pressed his mouth against mine, this time with full abandon and the force of a final goodbye. My entire body lit with flames that tingled through my skin.

"Can you get me to the door?" I asked, my voice a broken whisper in the tumult of the rocks crashing down.

His hands traced down the backs of my arms as he turned to face the door. His face turned stony. "However long it takes, however far I have to go, I will find you."

"Just hurry," I said, half-laughing, half-crying at the thought of leaving him here.

"Be smart," he said. "You can't go home. They'll find you and throw you back in here. Protect yourself, Vera. I will come for you."

"I know." I had to trust that in this one moment, he was telling me the truth. That all the lies were finally over. That even though he might be afraid, and even though he might think that he needed to pay for what he'd done, he would come through that door and not leave me alone forever.

"If that door doesn't lead to life, Vera, if it leads to a place even worse than this, I will still follow you through it. I would follow you through death itself."

I pressed another kiss to his lips and then scooted backward off his lap. I slipped from his grip and grabbed his hands. Together we stood.

"Will they hurt you?" I said, glancing at the monsters writhing outside the barrier of mist.

"They will try," he said. Then he shoved me toward the door.

21

My hand grabbed the knob and turned. Instantly, I was pouring through molten hot light so bright that my eyes burned even with my eyelids crammed shut. The pressure of Ash's fingers vanished from my back, and I hoped that wouldn't be the last time I ever felt his touch. I crashed through open space, though it wasn't exactly like falling. It was as if I was simply flying through the air.

A weight lifted off my chest and cracked as it fell away. I took a deep breath and then crashed into the ground. I rolled and grabbed my shoulder, rubbing where it was sore from the impact. When I opened my eyes, it took a moment for them to adjust.

I was in a forest. My entire body ached from an exhaustion unlike any I'd known before. At my feet was a worn, freestanding, blue door. I pushed my hands into the soft ground and quickly stood. Twigs and leaf fragments clung to my hair. I shook a few of them out and glanced around. I was outside of the Labyrinth, back at the exact place I'd stood before the mind mage had forced me in. That felt like an eternity ago, although it had only been a handful of days.

Staring at the door, I bent double and placed my hands on my knees. A week. How could it have only been one week?

Laughter behind me turned my attention from the Labyrinth. Edith and Ferrier stood several paces away, laughing and crying as they embraced in the cool shade of the forest.

They hadn't spotted me yet, distracted by their own elation. I pressed my knuckles to my lips and a laugh bubbled up inside me, followed immediately by sinking pain as heavy as the world itself.

I turned back to the door, reaching for it, my fingers brushing the rough, worn wood as my mind pictured the man I'd left behind it.

Curious, I peeked around the door. Nothing but more forest. I walked around the door and then stood facing it. My chest rocked with silent sobs, and this time, I didn't attempt to shut them away.

I vowed right then that I would never stop waiting for him, even if he never came. The monsters might have killed him, or it might take him years to free all of the Nameless within the Labyrinth from their madness, but I trusted him when he said he would come, and I wouldn't go back on my word.

After much cajoling, I'd lied to Edith and said I would stop waiting when two years had passed.

I carried a basket under my arm through the market in Ravlin, a town tucked far at the northern corner of Bevon, miles from Westburg and the king's castle. The early fall morning was crisp, and the sun felt good against my chilled skin. The vendors in the market had heaps of fresh corn, bumpy squash, and beautiful round tomatoes.

It had been two years and sixty-one days, and I still hadn't stopped waiting for Ash.

In that time, I'd listened for every scrap of news related to the Labyrinth. There were reports of mind mages disappearing, which meant they were likely still getting thrown into the miserable prison. Every time I heard the common myths of the Labyrinth whispered on the tongues of the townspeople and travelers, my shoulders tightened at the memory of that place and my heart sank at the knowledge that Ash might still be trapped. Or worse.

Edith perused the market stalls ahead, picking out a bolt of cloth to make a new dress. Ferrier was in school and doing quite well, considering the fears she'd had to overcome to even agree to enroll. Healing from the Labyrinth had taken time, and none of us was fully free from the nightmares that plagued us, but we'd found a new life in this small village.

I spotted Archer across the square and grinned widely, hurrying to where he stood outside the carpenter's shop. He dusted off his hands and welcomed a hug. I'd never apologized for hugging him after finding them again, and he never complained.

"I heard you come in late," he teased, pushing my shoulder with his knuckles.

I smirked. "We had a new member join last night."

His brows lifted and he leaned in, a conspiratorial tone to his voice. "Did you make him dance in circles and chant?"

"We don't do that sort of thing. We just...practice. It's nice to have a few mind mages to learn from and to teach. Danny said he's ready to come to a meeting."

Archer stood tall, his hands flat against his chest. A look of sadness was replaced quickly as fierce pride swept his face. "He's really...he's just..."

"I know," I said, crossing my arms. "He is."

Archer was a grown man now, and Danny was growing taller by the day. Archer had never manifested any magical abilities, but Danny had begun moving things with his mind just last year, and in that time, he'd come a long way in his focus and control of his magic. He still preferred to stay home with Mother, Archer, and me, so when he'd told me yesterday that he wanted to attend a meeting of our secret society, I was shocked—and thrilled.

Mother would be reluctant to let him. Her fear of the king discovering us hadn't waned in the two years we'd lived here, and she lived every day with jittery nerves and an increasingly distant demeanor. But I remembered the way she'd clapped a hand to her mouth and wrapped me in a crushing hug when I'd returned home. She wasn't the cruel woman I remembered. She had her faults, and her way of dealing with things was to avoid them—a trait I'd acquired—but my short stay in the Labyrinth had changed my perspective on things, and once I decided to be at peace with her, we'd gotten along just fine.

"I've got to get back to work. Just stepped out when I saw you," Archer said, heading back into the carpenter's shop.

The air smelled of the first sweet hint of fall and the abundance of the earth. I smiled at the colorful produce and ruddy faces as I strolled slowly through the market. The man hovering behind Edith stood with his hands clasped at his waist.

I grinned at the pair of them. Edith must have felt my stare because she glanced over her shoulder and flashed me a warm smile.

Then her face drooped—she read my thoughts almost too well sometimes. Every time I looked at Edith and her new husband, a pang of jealousy shot through me. I'd finally found my place in the world, training with the underground group of mind mages and working at the local bakery to supplement my family's income, but I still felt alone.

My family was all I'd ever thought I needed, and I'd choose to save my brothers again every time, but ever since leaving Ash behind, I'd realized I wanted more. I wanted to feel the way I had with his arms around me, fleeting as that had been.

"Is that the one you'd like?" The deep voice of the vendor behind the nearest market stall broke me out of my daydream.

My hand had been resting on a bumpy squash. I jerked my fingers off the vegetable.

"You're welcome to look," he said, his eyes sparking at me.

I looked away quickly, pretending to be interested in the pumpkins on the ground.

"Are you still waiting for him?" the man asked.

I sucked in a sharp breath and glanced back at Edith, who now carried a bolt of fabric in her basket. She moved her arm around her husband's waist, and they walked down the road together. My eyes snapped back to the vendor.

"Whoever he is, he's a lucky man. I just hope he doesn't leave you waiting much longer."

Everyone in this small town knew I was waiting for someone. It had come up often enough. Word had gotten around that Vera Rivers was not available. I had turned down an offer of marriage to one of the local farmers I'd come to know in passing in this little town, which seemed sensible at the time. I swallowed and picked up the squash along with two others and dug a few coins from my purse.

I tried to form a response, but no words came. I couldn't swallow the lump in my throat.

I nodded at him and turned back toward the bustling market, which suddenly felt very much like a maze. For a moment, my heart stuttered. This was a labyrinth all its own—the real world. I hadn't yet been able to manipulate reality the way I could in the prison Ash had built, as if what I'd done in that awful place had also been a lie. Or maybe his magic had made mine stronger.

I glanced down at the produce in my basket. No monsters fought to steal my life or my sanity in this town. And yet my sanity drained a little more every day that Ash didn't arrive. What if he wasn't even alive anymore and I was waiting for someone who was never coming? What if madness had finally taken him, and he was now a Nameless wandering in the Labyrinth of his own making?

My basket grew heavy, and I shifted it to my other arm. Just as I swung it around, I bumped into someone.

"Oh, my apologies," I said, as I stepped away.

An older gentleman I didn't recognize, a traveler by the look of his fancy suit, glanced over his shoulder. "No worries, my dear." He clasped his wife's hand against his arm, bowed politely to me, and moved along. As they walked away, I heard the man mutter, "The door doesn't work anymore. It's locked. The king will have to find a new prison."

My heart thunked against my ribs.

As my gaze lingered on them, I sensed someone watching me from across the market. I scanned the far row of vendor stalls with narrow eyes. Walking between two stalls on the other side of the road came a face that stole my breath.

I dropped my basket as I stared back at him.

When those deep brown eyes met mine, my entire world burst into vibrant color as sparkling mist erupted from my body and curled into the air. A gasp that was part laugh burst from my lips, and I broke into a run. His hands slipped from his pockets, and he too walked toward me.

Part of me feared he was an illusion, but when my arms wrapped around him and my chest crashed into his, he felt solid and real.

For a long moment, we stood in each other's embrace. My breaths alternated between crying and laughing, the pain of waiting for so long, rising and disappearing in a single moment.

By the time I pulled away, I felt many eyes in the market staring at us. I didn't care.

"There you are, Vera Rivers. I've been looking for you for weeks." He smiled down at me. "You did an excellent job hiding." His neatly trimmed chin tipped against the side of my head and I felt his heartbeat against my own. He felt stronger than when I'd left him in the Labyrinth two years ago.

And before I could say a single word, he cupped my face in his hands and brought his lips down to meet mine.

Thank you for reading *Labyrinth of Lies and Sacrifice*! Find bonus content from Ash's point of view by signing up to be a reader VIP here: www.cfeblack.com/pages/vip

Labyrinth of Lies and Sacrifice is the final book in the *Sacrificed Hearts* multi-author group series. These fantasy romance tales inspired by monsters of legend provide a sweet and swoony take on the Sacrificed to the Monster trope. Experience the magic today in the *Sacrificed Hearts* series, a collection of stand-alone short novels packed with enchanting romance, strong heroines, and sacrificial themes.

Explore the entire series here: https://everlyhaywood.com/sacrificedhearts/

Also by C. F. E. Black

Scepter and Crown series:
Shield of Shadow
Blade of Ash
Crown of Dust
Scepter of Fire

Secrets of the Fae:
The Starlit Prince
The Shadow Heir

Sacrificed Hearts series:
Labyrinth of Lies and Sacrifice

Other titles:
The Veritas Project

Sign up to be a reader VIP at
www.cfeblack.com/vip

If you enjoyed this book, please consider leaving a review.
It helps more than you know.

Acknowledgements

We did it! The final book in the Sacrificed Hearts series has entered the world. Thank you to Tara and Everly for running such an amazing group! I'm thankful I got to write alongside all of you: Tara, Everly, Callie, Deborah, and Mary. Y'all were a blast to work with, and I'm honored to have written this series with you all.

Sarah KL Wilson, you're the reason for this book! Thank you, friend, for everything.

Thanks, Callie, for always being there for a laugh and a bucketload of encouragement.

Thank you to my beta readers for improving this book in the ways I didn't even know it needed. And to my editor, Sara Lawson, for all your wisdom. You know what I mean to say better than I do! Also, to Myriah, for polishing this and catching all the little things the rest of us missed.

To Will, for supporting me as an author, even though it means the laundry is never really finished and on deadline weeks I'm a bit of a basket case. To my boys, for bringing me such joy every day. I love my two little dirt-loving bookworms.

And thank you to all my readers. Thank you for giving this book a try! Your messages and support mean more than you know.

Finally, thank you, Lord, for teaching me what it means to die to myself so that I can truly live. Thank you for setting me free. As always, soli Deo gloria.

C. F. E. Black loves to get swept away in books, both reading and writing them. Fantasy and science fiction have been her bread and butter since childhood, and she can't imagine life without her beloved fictional worlds. She lives in beautiful north Alabama with her superhero husband, sons, and fur-family. Connect with her and explore her books at www.cfeblack.com.